THE

LAST

SONG

OF

ORPHEUS

THE
LAST
SONG
OF
ORPHEUS

ROBERT SILVERBERG

SUBTERRANEAN PRESS 2010

First Edition

ISBN
978-1-59606-310-5

Subterranean Press
PO Box 190106
Burton, MI 48519

www.subterraneanpress.com

For Barry Malzberg

NOW STRIKE THE golden lyre. Bring forth a ringing chord. Another, louder. Louder yet: a chord to raise the dead. Yes, even that: death itself cannot withstand your music. So strike the lyre; raise the dead; make the rivers weep, Orpheus, and the trees shed their leaves in sorrow.

And strike another chord, an even louder one. Then a softer one, and softer still.

Sing, Orpheus!

Sing of your life, and of the understanding of sacred things that has been given to you, and of the tasks the gods have laid upon you, and of your sufferings in pursuit of those tasks, and of your death. And of the eternal renewal that follows death.

Sing!

2

two

T HIS WILL BЄ my last song, which I make for you, Musaeus my son, telling all there is to tell of my life. My last song, but also my first, for in my end is my beginning, and for me there are no ends and no beginnings but only the circle that is eternity. My sense of time and space is not like yours, for I know, better than you, better than any mortal possibly could, that the serpent, Time, curves round upon itself and grasps its tail in its mouth. I stand outside; I contain everything; I perceive the alpha and the omega and for me they do not have the same order of being and arrangement that they do for you. Past, present, future: for me, as for all those who are in whole or in part divine, they are all one indisseverable thing. My yesterdays are my tomorrows, my tomorrows are my yesterdays. It is decreed that I must forever reenact my past, which is indistinguishable from my future, both of them constituting an eternal present. I have lived, and I have died, and I have lived again, and I have died again, and so it will be, repeated and repeated and repeated, world without end.

If I tell you things that you already know, forgive me, for the gods deem it necessary that you hear them again.

I am Orpheus, the son of Apollo. At least it is said that he was my father. I will not deny it. But also people say that my father was Oeagros, king of Thrace, who ruled over the rough unlettered Ciconian folk, and I do not deny that either. I deny nothing; I confirm nothing. But I can at least tell you that beyond any question my mother was the the muse Calliope. It was she who taught me how to make verses to be sung, and Apollo who gave me my golden lyre, which Hermes fashioned for me with his own hands. And so music has flowed from me all my life as though from an inextinguishable fountain, which is to say that there has been music in the world since the beginning of time and that music will endure to time's end, and beyond it to the moment of beginning again.

I was only a boy when Apollo came to me with that lyre. Not truly young, you understand—I was never young, just as I will never be old—but this was in the time of my life when I was a boy. I lived in Thrace at the court of my father King Oeagros, and the life I led was that of any youthful prince, that is to say, hunting and mastering the games, and attending the rites and sacrifices and later helping to take part in them, and learning how to handle a sword and a spear and a little about the making of verses and the setting of them to music. My father was a rough, remote, thick-bearded man, strong and grim, as kings often are. I was not his only son and he and I spoke very infrequently, though he was as kind to me as he was capable of being. He had dedicated himself to the god Dionysus and we often performed the turbulent rites appropriate to that god, the torchlight festivals and the slaughter of beasts and the chanting of songs and the drinking of wine, and sometimes also the drinking of blood.

Of my mother Calliope I saw very little. She did not dwell at court, but from time to time I was told that she had come to see me, and I went to a cave in the forest that was considered a sacred place to receive her motherly embrace. She was tall and beautiful, very beautiful indeed, a full-breasted bright-eyed woman with long lustrous hair, and there was a special radiance about her that told me even at a time when I understood almost nothing at all that she must be of divine origin. But it remained finally for my nurse to reveal to me that she was one of the nine muses, who were the daughters of Zeus and Mnemosyne, and that like many of her sisters she went among mortals from time to time and lay with them and bore children by them, so that the special gifts of the Muses would pass from the Olympians to the race of mankind. Thus she had lured Oeagros to this cave on a day of lightning and torrential rain when he had been hunting and needed sudden shelter, and there she had given herself to him, and I was the product of that union. So said my nurse, at any rate. That was a wondrous moment for me, when I was told that my mother was divine and that I was the grandchild of Zeus.

But there was a greater revelation to come, not very long afterward. I was pursuing a boar in the forest on a dark day when the clouds hung low and thick. As I ran through a dense glade a voice out of nowhere spoke my name, a quiet voice that nevertheless was as commanding as the voice of a hundred kings.

"Orpheus," it said, and I halted and turned, stunned, and from between two mighty oak trees came a slender golden-haired man of such beauty that I knew him at once to be a god. In his hands he held a lyre of extraordinary workmanship, and I could see the horns of a second lyre rising behind him, strapped to his back. In that same gentle and amazing voice he said, "I have a gift for you, Orpheus."

He handed me the lyre. I had had a lyre of my own from my earliest years, and fancied that I played it with some skill, but I had never seen a lyre like this one. Its soundbox was a tortoise shell, but a shell of such beauty and perfection of pattern as is unknown in this world, and its frame was not of wood but of gold; and as for its strings—there were seven of them—they were golden too, as were the pegs to which they were affixed. I held my hand above them and my fingers trembled.

"Go on," the stranger said. "Touch them!"

At his command I touched them—I had always used only my fingertips, never a plectrum, with my lyres—and from it came such a sound as made my heart quiver and lurch in my breast.

There is no sound like the sound of the lyre. It does not pierce one's ears like the sound of the flute, nor does it shake the hills like a properly struck drum, nor set the heart atremble with warlike impulses like the cry of the trumpet. But it achieves other things, and they are great things, for it is perfect for the accompaniment of the human voice, fitting the contours of the singing tone the way a woman's body fits a man's.

The subtle shadings of its tone are unmatched in their beauty, and in the hands of a master the lyre catches the listener's heart and holds it in an unshakeable grasp. The moment I touched this new lyre that the god had given me—for I had no doubt that this was a god—I knew that I would be such a master, and that all the world would yield before the power of my playing.

"It is for you," he said. "It is the work of Hermes, and there is only one other of its sort in the world." Which he took now from his shoulders; and he stroked its strings in a loving way and brought from them a music that was like no music mortal ears had ever heard.

In one staggering moment I came to understand that I must be in the presence of bright-shining Apollo himself, and that in some sense I was his son as well as that of Oeagros. He played a melody and nodded to me and I played an answering one, and he smiled—until you have seen the smile of Apollo, you have no understanding of what a smile can be—and he answered my hesitant line with a flourish of his own, to which I replied more boldly, gathering strength and confidence with each movement of my fingers against those golden cords, so that after a time the music that was coming from me was nearly as potent as the one he was offering me. And for a long while we stood there in the secret glade, playing one to another, until I was no longer sure which one of us was Orpheus and which, Apollo.

Then he capped our song with a final flourish and all was silent and I was only Orpheus again, but an Orpheus forever transformed.

"Now you know who you are and who you will be," he said.

And, yes, it was true: I was Orpheus, the maker of songs. Great Apollo came to me often in that forest and instructed me in the art of melody so that what came from my lyre could touch the heart even of a stone, and when I went to my mother Calliope in her cave she taught me the secrets of making verses that would hold people entranced the way a magical spell might hold them; and so it was that a shaggy-haired Thracian princeling entered into his role in the universe.

It is the music that makes me essential: that makes me, indeed, the demigod that I am. Through it I help the cosmos make sense of itself. Music is the divine mathematics. My songs, my quartets, my symphonies, my merest scrap of melody, all are needed in order to sustain the underlying clarity by which all is held together. I am indispensable. Zeus, speaking through Apollo, has made that quite clear to me, as I will tell in a moment. There is that which is mortal in me but also there is that which is godly. Like all mortals, I have been born and I have suffered and I have died, but like all gods I have existed from the beginning, unchangeable and eternal.

The music sees me through the suffering, and I have known plenty of that. That painful Eurydice business, for example: the worst, of course, ugly, stupid, unpardonable nonsense, through which I must pass again and again. I failed her in her moment of need, but of course that was not by my choice. The least forgivable sins we commit are the needless ones. Certainly I thought it needless to let her die the second time, but the gods did not agree, and who am I to question their decrees? Common sense said that when I was bringing her forth out of the land of the dead I should never have looked back at her after having been warned not to do so—certainly not I, who knew the consequences, because to me all directions are the same direction and what lies ahead for me also lies behind. Yet I did look back, for it was decreed that I must, and she perished once more, this time forever, and my heart was riven. And is riven again and again, for it happens again and again, and I grieve, and I sing of my grief, and my love is born again, and dies again, and dies the second time again, and so it will be, world without end. Just as the bloody thing with the Bacchantes must happen again and again and again. I see the end, I see the beginning. They will come for me, they will tear me apart, I will die. And in my end is my beginning.

3

Chree

THESE THINGS THAT I have just said I learned
gradually, over the years; for even though my spirit
moves freely through all of time and space, and almost in
the manner of a god I can see both forward and backward
through all that has occurred and all that is yet to come, even
so I am capable of learning things; indeed, my whole life has
been a process of learning that which must be learned. If you
see any paradox in that, so be it: what is a paradox to the
mind of men is the root of eternal truth to the gods.

I was a master of music from the moment Apollo placed
that lyre in my hands. But I was young yet, and not given to
reflection even upon my own mastery, so it was necessary for
Apollo to come to me in a dream and teach me the higher
mysteries of my art.

He took me up in his chariot high above the sky, where in that great lofty-vaulted darkness I could see the planets in their courses and hear the cosmic music that they made as they traveled on their unalterable routes. "Listen," he commanded me. "Hear them sing!"

My mind was opened and all the universe came rushing in. And the sound that it made was the most glorious music I had ever heard. It was a thousand thousand lyres resounding at once, and the voice of ten thousand thousand throats in the purest harmony.

And indeed I understood that the curving paths of the moving worlds were like the strings of a gigantic lyre. More than that: strict harmonic laws governed the sounds that came from them. From Earth to the Moon there was an interval of a tone; from the Moon to Mercury, a semi-tone, and another semi-tone from Mercury to Venus. From Venus to the Sun, a minor third; from the Sun to Mars, a tone; from Mars to Jupiter, a semi-tone; from Jupiter to Saturn, a semi-tone; and from Saturn out to the sphere of the stars, a minor third, everything blending together in a perfect harmony. All this, under Apollo's guidance, I heard with my own ears. The music was true and real. And everything was in perfect order: the cosmic harmony governed all, and kept the cosmos from falling into mere chaos. Music is a beautiful concord beween different sounds, and the universe is a harmonious mathematical structure that the far-seeing gods designed according to the same perfect unbending rules, the right relationship of one thing to another, all things bound up in one harmony.

"Now, Orpheus," said Apollo, when I had caught my breath and begun to encompass within my mind the new things that were pouring into it, "see, if you will, how the laws of music are the same as the laws that rule the cosmos."

He asked me what governed the sounds that the strings of my lyre made, and after a long moment's thought I replied that the tuning was controlled not by the thickness of the cords or by the materials from which they were fashioned nor the tension with which they are strung, but by a set of proportions reflecting the length of the strings. Strings under the same tension, I said, are stopped differently to sound different notes, according to the ratios 2:1 for the octave, 3:2 for the fifth, and 4:3 for the third, and so forth. "Yes," Apollo said. "This is true. And the tuning of the worlds? Is that not the same? Listen to their music, Orpheus! Listen to it! The heavens themselves follow the laws of number that your lyre obeys!"

And so they did. I felt a kind of ecstasy spread through me as I seized upon the understanding that music was not just a series of pleasant sounds, but the epitome in sound of the balance and order of the universe. That music and that order are the work of the One God whom men know by many names, by which everything is connected to everything, issuing forth the endless continuous song that is the harmony of the cosmos.

My dream went on and on. Apollo showed me much else, things that I may not share with you in any detail, for they border on the Great Mysteries that only an initiate in the highest order may know. I will tell you that he revealed to me planets not yet known to the wisest sages of Hellas, ice-shrouded worlds that lie far out beyond Saturn, but are subject to the same laws that govern those we know. He took me up into the domain of the blazing stars and taught me things about them that would astonish you, if I dared reveal them here. I heard their song also. The star-song would make you weep if you could hear it, so beautiful is it, so noble. He took me down then into the realm of the infinitely small, where the same musical laws prevail that dictate the motions of the planets and the stars. By the time he was done with me I was numb with joy, and my head swam with wonder at the grandeur of the great creator-god whom we have called by so many names.

Then I awakened and looked about me, gasping in amazement at the memory of all that I had seen. My head was full of swirls of blazing light—the myriad colors of the fiery stars, the radiance of the planets—but above all it swam with the blessed music of the spheres, a music that would stay with me always.

From that moment on the doorway to true knowledge lay open to me. I knew the nature of the divine framework that our world and all the other worlds are strung upon, and realized that it was my task to bring the heavenly harmonies down to our world through my playing and my singing, to maintain the reason and beauty and wholeness that are Apollo through the art of music, and thus to sustain my portion of the great harmonic structure. And it became clear to me that in the proper performance of my task I must travel widely, and suffer greatly, and strive unendingly, and give my life again and again, for the sake of helping to uphold the miraculous structure that the gods have built.

4

four

I WILL TRY TO tell the tale in what you, poor mortal Musaeus, would think of as the proper fashion, a beginning, a middle, an end, although you must attempt to understand that for me such concepts have very little meaning.

I will tell, all in proper order, of my visit to Egypt, and of my kingship in Thrace, and my voyage to Colchis with the Argonauts, and of such other things as are harmonious parts of my tale. But I should begin with the story of Orpheus and Eurydice, since that is the one for which I am best known.

That story begins when I was still only an idle wandering princeling and maker of pretty songs. A time came when the gods decided that I needed to know love, which until then had been absent from my life. Nobler music was required of me than I as yet had the art to create, and for that it was necessary for me to experience love. Love, after all, is the great force that drives creation, and what can be more important to the gods than creation, which is the reason for their own existence? How could I sing of love without knowing it? For me to sing of it in a true way I needed to know what it was, truly to know, and so the gods in their infinite wisdom led me to Eurydice. And the gods decreed also that I had to learn not only love but the suffering that comes with the loss of one's beloved, and to experience the redemption that comes after the most acute and profound pain.

So the gods gave me Eurydice; or, rather, they placed Eurydice in my path and caused me to choose her, although I believed then that I was choosing her of my own free will. Let us say that I did choose her of my own free will, since I know that there are those who believe that such a thing as free will actually exists in this universe. Why, then, you might ask me, would I choose Eurydice, above all other women?

And I would tell you that I perceived her as song made flesh, and there is nothing I love more than song.

5

five

ERYDICE WAS THE daughter of King Creon, not the Creon who would one day be king in Thebes at the time when Oedipus was there, but another and earlier one, who ruled on the shores of the swift-flowing river Peneius in the green and lovely valley of Tempe that lies between Olympus and Ossa. He had promised her in marriage to Aristaeus, who is said by some to be one of Apollo's many sons. Of that paternity I know nothing, nor can I tell you anything of the man, and certainly nothing good; but I do know that this Aristaeus was one who traveled widely, visiting such places as Sardinia and Sicily, and had several wives and begot a number of sons, and even had paid a call at my own Thrace and been initiated into the Mysteries of Dionysus. But all that happened long after he caught the eye of Creon and was affianced to that king's daughter. If the gods were more gentle than they are, he would have married Eurydice as her father intended and they would perhaps have grown old together and been fated to be forgotten entirely by the makers of songs and plays. But the gods are not gentle.

So it came to pass that I happened to be traveling through Tempe at the time of the betrothal of Eurydice and Aristaeus and sang at their betrothal-feast. Perhaps she bore no great love for Aristaeus, or, very probably, none at all; but like an obedient daughter she was fully intent on the marriage until the moment that her eye fell on me, and mine on her.

I had sung often enough before that time of the shafts of Eros, and how they strike people all unawares and transform their lives in an instant. But until that moment my verses of Eros were mere verses, as any songmaker will make from time to time out of the materials that lie readily at hand, whether he has had experience of their meaning or not. Now everything changed. Eros, that wild boy with golden wings, who shows no respect for anything but the wanton commands of his mother Aphrodite, and sometimes does not respect even those, flew down upon us and pierced us both with his barbed arrows. The shaft made its way deep into my breast like a red-hot rod. It sent an intense throbbing sensation coursing through me, as painful as it was pleasurable, that kindled an unquenchable conflagration instantly within me. Eurydice's sudden gasp told me that she had been struck as well; and Eurydice and I looked upon each other and I felt what I felt and she felt what she felt and in that moment the marriage of Aristaeus and Eurydice was brought to its end before it had even begun.

Her father was troubled when she bore the news to him, for he knew that to disrupt a betrothal was a serious matter that often had somber consequences. But he was neither unwise nor cruel, and would not force her into a loveless match; and so Aristaeus was dismissed and the new betrothal was announced.

Like any fond lover I believed that Eurydice was the fairest of all women, the equal of golden Aphrodite herself, and I made songs that said just that, knowing that Aphrodite would understand that I spoke as lovers speak and would not bear a grudge against my Eurydice for my rash comparison. In truth I have never beheld Aphrodite, but if she is more beautiful than my Eurydice was, she is beautiful indeed. For Eurydice was tall and slender, with gleaming golden hair and a delicate rosy bloom in her cheeks and skin softer than the silk the women wear in the empire of the yellow-skinned folk, and eyes of a brilliance and a clarity and a sheen that even a goddess might envy, and there was nothing about her that was not perfect. Thus I made the first song of Orpheus and Eurydice, which told of the accident of our meeting and the power of Eros' shaft and the delight of our new love; and I think it is the happiest of all songs ever made. Certainly it is the happiest of mine.

But, as I say, the gods are not gentle. Bleak omens hovered over our marriage from the start. At the wedding, the torch that the priest of Hymen carried smoked and sputtered, fouling the air and bringing tears to the eyes of all the guests. Old Creon tried to make light of it, telling us that the omen was propitious, that these were tears of joy. But I knew better, and, I am sure, so did he.

If I had taken my bride back to Thrace at once, perhaps all would have been well. But that was not how things were meant to be. Thus King Creon asked us to tarry awhile at his court before we took our leave, and I agreed, and Eurydice and I lived in his palace as man and wife and in her arms I tasted all the joys that you mortals know so well. Everything was exactly as I knew it would be, and nevertheless each day was a fresh time of surprise and wonder. That is the paradox of my life, that I march constantly onward into that which is ordained for me and which I have experienced so many times before, and as each event befalls me it is both new and old, a recapitulation that is also a discovery.

AND all during that time the brooding Aristaeus, that dark and lustful man, was lurking in the woods nearby, nursing the wound of his rejection and planning his revenge. One morning when Eurydice was wandering in the meadows with her maids, he emerged from a thicket and seized her by the arm, and would have flung her down and taken her then and there. The maids clustered close, shrieking at him and pummeling him, and Eurydice wrested herself free of him and ran. But it was all to no avail, for in her frantic flight she trod upon a venomous serpent nesting hidden in the grass, and was bitten on the ankle and perished in a moment.

I have never felt so much like a mortal as I did in the hour when her maids came to me, bearing lifeless Eurydice. With her I had experienced the wondrous ecstasies of love and now I experienced the bitter pain of grief. These are mortal things;

and whatever part of me is mortal was shaken by them the way a tree is shaken in the storms of winter.

So I put away my bright wedding clothes and donned the black cloak of mourning, and as the flames of her funeral pyre rose toward the heavens I sang a dirge for my lost Eurydice that brought torrents of rain from the sky; but the fire burned on and on even so, until the last of my Eurydice was consumed and I was left alone with my despair.

I could find nothing to console me for my loss, neither in the philosophies of Egypt nor in the serene wisdom of Apollo nor even in my own music. Distraught, I drifted from land to land, singing the sad song of lost Eurydice over and again. But my singing gave me no solace. Nor was it welcomed by others. I wept, and everyone about me wept also. I cast such a pall of gloom over all who heard me that men feared my coming, and word traveled ahead of me that all should flee, for the bleak-hearted Orpheus was approaching, singing a song that would rend the heart of any listener just as the death of Eurydice had rent his own. They say the gods themselves wept for me. They say even rocks shed tears at the sound of my lyre, and the sorrowing trees cast their leaves to the ground even in the green days of summer. Of weeping rocks and grieving trees I will tell you nothing. There are many stories that are told about me. I do not confirm; I do not deny.

Then one day a nymph appeared before me—a messenger from Zeus, surely, a shimmering golden beam of sunlight breaking through my darkness—and said, "You are so foolish, Orpheus, roaming about like this constantly singing your somber song. What good does such a song serve? The woman you loved is dead, yes. But you will not bring her back with a song like that."

I knew the part I was meant to play in this little colloquy. Dutifully I said, "What kind of song, then, should I sing?"

"A song to soften the hearts of those who keep her now," replied the nymph. "A song of the sort that only Orpheus can sing. Go to the Netherworld, Orpheus. Sing for Hades and his wife Persephone. Enchant them into restoring your bride. It is the only way. Strike your lyre, Orpheus! Plead for her return! Ask the gods of the Netherworld to relent, and they will! They will!"

6

six

THE NETHERWORLD HAS many gates, but the one that was best for my purpose was situated at Tainaron in the far southern Peloponnese, which is a back entrance to Tartarus close by the palace of King Hades and Queen Persephone, and that was where I made my descent. The preparation for the journey took me many days. One does not go lightly into the Netherworld. I fasted; I bathed; I sequestered myself in a house of fire and steam and sat by the heat until every pore of mine had opened. Then I went to the sacred grove of Persephone and dug a trench and sacrificed a young ram and a black ewe to the Queen of Hell, and their blood ran down into the earth and was received below. I felt the cold wind blowing upward

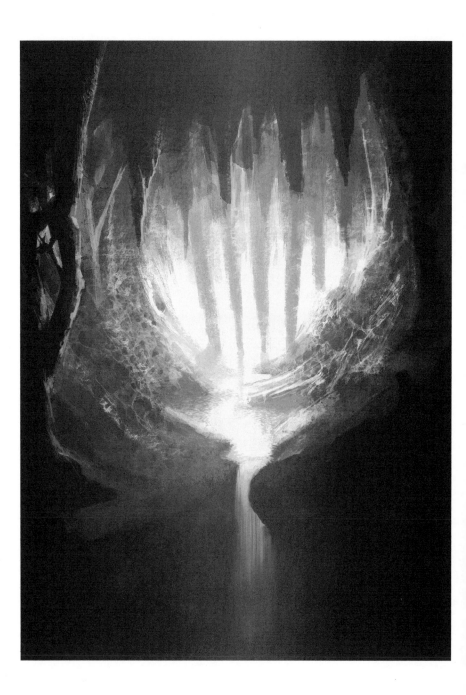

toward me out of the kingdom of Hades and the gate opened for me.

The road into Hades' realm is a difficult one, a baffling circuitous path of innumerable branches and forks that leads down into that infinite pit, that great gulf that has neither bottom nor foundation. It is necessary for the souls of the newly dead to be accompanied by guides as they proceed to whatever last resting place awaits them. But the journey was familiar to me, for I knew that I had made it many times in cycles past, though this was, as ever, the first of them. Unerringly I chose the correct forks, and I swam the river of blood and the river of weeping, holding my lyre high above my head as I swam, and onward through that shadowy realm of the dead I went until I came to the shores of the Styx, which is a river that no one can cross unaided, for its black waters are poisonous; and I waited there beside the barren bank of that chilly stream until the grim ferryman, seeing what he took to be a newly arrived soul on the bank, came rowing toward me.

"Take me across, Charon," I said.

He gave me a cold, cold look. Hell's ferryman was a huge brawny man, uncouth and filthy, with matted hair and a coarse tangled beard. His body was powerful, broad-shouldered and deep-chested, with great muscles that rippled and swelled with every stroke of his oar. He wore only a soiled, tattered rag about his loins and his eyes were as cold and hard as ice. "Who are you to come to Hell while breath still is in you?" he demanded, resting on his pole. "It is not given to those who live to enter here."

By way of reply I unslung my lyre and struck a gentle chord, and told him that so long as my dear one had been deprived of life I could no longer be said to be alive myself, for my heart was dead within me. Orpheus of Thrace am I, I said, the musician, the beloved of bright-shining Apollo, and I sang to him of the love of Orpheus for Eurydice, and of her cruel death and her husband's grief, and from the way that I sang even that formidable ferryman could see at once that I was that very Orpheus. He knew then, for it was foretold as everything is foretold, why I had come, and his icy eyes clouded over, and the muscles of his jaws worked with turmoil and pain. For Charon is forbidden by the gods' decree to ferry the living across the Styx and, knowing what I was about to ask of him, every fiber of his being was bristling with the desire to refuse my request. But he could not refuse. Zeus himself had sent a messenger to tell me to come here. Taking me across was forbidden, and yet he could not refuse. In the toils of that conflict the ferryman was hopelessly lost, and he stood before me irresolute, baffled, angry.

I sang my songs and my singing began to melt through his bewilderment. I told him that Eurydice had been taken before her time—it was not true, of course, since nothing can ever happen before its time—and that I was here to plead with the gods of the Netherworld to release her to me. And as I saw his dour expression beginning to soften, my singing grew in fervor, until I was singing once again with the irresistible beauty that had been at my command before her death and which I had not been able to recover since that dark day.

My playing worked its force upon him. The ferryman closed his eyes a moment and let his clenched muscles loosen their grip. Then he shrugged a shrug of resignation and beckoned me aboard his boat and rowed me quickly to the other bank.

Cerberus, the three-headed dog that the monster Echidna spawned when she lay with the monster Typhon, was waiting for me there, crouching before the inner gate. He is a savage frightful thing, is Cerberus, all yellow fangs and writhing snaky hair, and it is a wonder that the spirits of the newly dead do not perish again with fright at their first sight of that awful hound. But it is not the task of Cerberus to rebuff the newly dead; it is living intruders like me whom he must guard against, and as I approached him his hackles rose and his jowls quivered and blazing spittle splashed from his three terrible mouths. From him came a ferocious growl, in truth three growls emerging from them together, each at a different clashing pitch so that they set up a sound most dire and harsh. But I had no fear of him. I played for him and sang to him and he paused in mid-growl, seemingly perplexed, and his great body, which had been tense and poised for a leap, slumped back in a posture of ease, and as I continued to sing his eyelids began to droop and he lowered one head and then another and then the third, and soon he lay with chins against the ground, sleeping as pleasantly as any happy puppy. I walked around him and went on my way.

What else can I tell you of my journey toward the monarchs of the Netherworld?

Beyond that gate I entered the Asphodel Fields, where those who in life were neither virtuous nor evil congregate and the souls of dead warriors twitter aimlessly like bats at sundown. With my lyre held before me I came to the ominous grove of black poplars, those joyless trees that signify the bleakness of this gloomy realm, which I had sung of often enough the way I had sung of love before I had ever known it.

Onward from there I went to the lofty white cypress, Queen Persephone's sacred tree, beneath whose spectral shade hordes of bloodless, nearly transparent ghosts gather to drink at the pool of forgetfulness before they are sent onward to their last dwelling-place. On the far side of it I came to the place of torment where the impious Ixion eternally pushes his heavy wheel in a circle and the vultures gnaw forever at the liver of that miserable giant Tityus and the ever-toiling Sisyphus fruitlessly rolls his huge stone uphill, only to see it tumble back again. All these, caught up in the strains of the melody I played, paused in their preoccupations to stare at me as I went past.

I sang to them. Oh, did I sing!

The bloodless ghosts wept as they heard me, and wheel-bound Ixion ceased his pushing, and Sisyphus too halted in his endless task to listen, and even Tityus' vultures looked up from their bloody work to give me what must be, for vultures, a glance of compassion. The inexorable Furies themselves, those hideous crones with black bat-wings and bloodshot eyes and the heads of dogs, stopped their vengeful shrieking and came almost timidly up beside me to touch the hem of my robe. Tears were rolling down their shriveled cheeks.

"Come with us," these grim sisters said, and, gamboling ahead of me like a pack of cheerful schoolgirls, led me through the meadows until the gates of Hades' royal palace rose before me.

Queen Persephone herself received me. I was grateful for that, for softening the heart of her pitiless husband would have been a much harder task. But Persephone knows what it is like to be swept off into Tartarus in the prime of one's youth, for she herself, the happy daughter of Demeter who brings fruitfulness to the fields, was carried away by stark Hades as she played in the green fields to be his queen in the infernal regions.

"I am Orpheus," I said. "You know why I am here."

"Yes. You seek your wife."

I gave her no chance then to tell me that I could not have her. I knew I had to reach her heart before she could utter any word of prohibition. Wielding my lyre as Zeus wields his thunderbolts, I wove a spell of song around the dark world's queen. I sang her the song of the love of Orpheus and Eurydice and I sang her the song of the death of Eurydice and I sang her the song of my despair and my wanderings and the song of my hope of a reunion, and I implored her, in the name of that aspect of God that goes by the name of Love, to restore her to me, so that once again I could go through the world singing of love's wonder and joy.

I KNEW I had won my case. There had to be some shred of pity in her, queen of Hell though she was, and there was. Even if it had not been foretold, I would have known that my music had moved her, for I could see a flush come to her lovely cheeks, as though she were thinking of what her life had been like in her happy youth in the fields of Demeter before cold Hades had come for her in his black chariot.

She said, because it was necessary for her to say it, "Orpheus, surely you must know that the dead may not leave here once they have come."

"I know that. I ask you to make an exception, O Queen. I implore you: release her from your husband's cold grasp." And I struck my lyre again, quickly recapitulating the themes of each song, the song of love, the song of death, the song of mourning, the song of yearning for reunion with my beloved. "Her time will come again, for she is mortal, and Tartarus will have her once more," I told her. "But she was taken too soon."

"You know that that is untrue."

"I do," I admitted. "But I beg you to let me have her until she grows old. And then she will be yours again."

Sadly she shook her head, and said that that was impossible. But I could see from her eyes that our words were only a ritual, that in fact we were playing out a conversation that would end in her capitulation.

"If you will not release her," I said, "then I will not return from this place alone. And so you will have my death as well as hers."

But it is not my destiny ever to die, at least insofar as death is most commonly understood, and Queen Persephone knew that. With a little sighing sound she turned to one of her handmaidens and asked that Eurydice be brought forth; and shortly forth she came slowly forward out of that group of newly arrived spirits by the pool of forgetfulness beside the white cypress.

She was limping a little, for the injury to her foot had not yet healed, and she was very pale, and her eyes, that had been so bright and clear, had the dull hopeless look of death in them. But I knew that she still had not tasted the waters of forgetfulness, for a look of shock and surprise came upon her face as she saw me, and she trembled and wept and came

running in her limping way toward me and flung herself into my arms.

I held her while she sobbed.

"Oh, Orpheus, have you also died?" she asked, at last. And I told her that I lived, and that I had come to fetch her out of Tartarus, for by special favor of the gods she would live again as well. As I spoke I looked beyond her to Queen Persephone, and begged her with my eyes, and the Queen of Tartarus said, "Yes. She is yours."

Just at that moment, of course, that stark monarch Hades emerged from some chamber deeper within the palace and, knowing at once what had taken place among us, glowered at the two of us and at his queen in a cold fury, and for a moment I thought all was lost. But Persephone turned upon her husband a look of such tender supplication that even the frigid heart of King Hades was melted by it. For a time he stood silent, unrelenting, intractable, but one could see that gradually his stern resolve was falling away; and in the end he yielded, with a brusque nod of approval, to his wife's request. Eurydice had his leave to depart from his kingdom.

But it would not be as simple as that, as anyone might have anticipated. He said, in a voice as black as the blackest night, "There is a condition, Orpheus."

Yes. It was no surprise. The gods are not gentle, and this one is the least gentle of them all. And I knew that he would attach a condition, and what that condition would be.

He is a terrifying deity, Hades is: black-bearded, sharp-featured, with a hard, cold face and dark eyes that flash like lightning. Like his brothers Zeus and Poseidon he is of towering stature and strength, and like them he bears himself with

running in her limping way toward me and flung herself into my arms.

I held her while she sobbed.

"Oh, Orpheus, have you also died?" she asked, at last. And I told her that I lived, and that I had come to fetch her out of Tartarus, for by special favor of the gods she would live again as well. As I spoke I looked beyond her to Queen Persephone, and begged her with my eyes, and the Queen of Tartarus said, "Yes. She is yours."

Just at that moment, of course, that stark monarch Hades emerged from some chamber deeper within the palace and, knowing at once what had taken place among us, glowered at the two of us and at his queen in a cold fury, and for a moment I thought all was lost. But Persephone turned upon her husband a look of such tender supplication that even the frigid heart of King Hades was melted by it. For a time he stood silent, unrelenting, intractable, but one could see that gradually his stern resolve was falling away; and in the end he yielded, with a brusque nod of approval, to his wife's request. Eurydice had his leave to depart from his kingdom.

But it would not be as simple as that, as anyone might have anticipated. He said, in a voice as black as the blackest night, "There is a condition, Orpheus."

Yes. It was no surprise. The gods are not gentle, and this one is the least gentle of them all. And I knew that he would attach a condition, and what that condition would be.

He is a terrifying deity, Hades is: black-bearded, sharp-featured, with a hard, cold face and dark eyes that flash like lightning. Like his brothers Zeus and Poseidon he is of towering stature and strength, and like them he bears himself with a regal presence befitting his power in the universe. Every aspect of him is frightening. But would one expect any softer look for the lord of the land of the dead? If I had not been born without fear I would have fallen to my knees before him. But I stood firm. Without releasing Eurydice, who stood coiled trembling against me, I stared steadily at him and awaited the pronouncing of the sentence.

I could go, he said.

I was free to make the journey upward into the land of the living, and Eurydice could go with me.

I must not turn to look at her, though. Not the slightest backward glance until we reached the upper air, or he would reclaim her in that instant and never relinquish her again.

Well, yes: it was as I expected. Nor did I dare quarrel with his decree. One does not negotiate with the king of Hell. I offered proud Hades my thanks, and made my grateful obeisance to gracious Queen Persephone, and turned from them, with Eurydice at my side, to begin the journey to the world of living men and women.

7

seven

WE SAID NOTHING as we set out on our way. The foggy haze of death still swirled about her spirit, and as for me, I moved as though moving within a dream. In the early stages of the journey I neither spoke nor touched my lyre's strings; scarcely did I do so much as think. Onward we walked, Eurydice always following a few paces behind me; and though the denizens of the Netherworld peered at us with a kind of blank-eyed curiosity as we passed, I did not meet their glances, nor did I pay heed to the idle questions they called out to us.

So I retraced my steps, past the place of torments, where all was proceeding once more as it would through eternities to come, and past the white cypress and its pool of forgetfulness, and the black poplars in whose crooked branches black birds of evil omen perched, glaring at us with their glinting yellow eyes, and in time we came to the ferryman's place at the bank of the Styx, where somber Charon had put me ashore at the outset of my mission.

He was nowhere to be seen, for he has no reason to wait for passengers on this side of the river; but I brought out my lyre and let some notes drift off into the mists that lay low over the black waters, and in time I heard the sound of his oars, and his boat came slowly toward us through the darkness.

If he felt any surprise at seeing us there, he showed no sign. In his dour way he beckoned, and I climbed into the boat and heard Eurydice clamber in behind me, and we stood, one behind the other, as he took us to the other side.

There we disembarked and left Charon and his boat behind, and started off on the road back to life.

All was night here. Apollo's heavenly light does not reach the realm of Hades, of course, but the places where the shades dwell have a certain dim glow of their own. Here there was none of that, only the dire emptiness that is the frontier of the kingdom of Hell, and a clammy dankness and a stale reek. But by the mercy of everloving Zeus I was able to see the signs of my own earlier track, the faint glimmering glow that my sandals had left when I made my way inward, and I was able to follow those faint clues as I proceeded toward the surface of the world.

Could Eurydice see those same signs, I wondered, and was she able to follow me as I went? Or would she lose sight of me and wander away from me in that multitude of branching forks?

Now and again I heard some small sound that told me she was still behind me, a soft sigh, a little gasp of discomfort as she touched her wounded heel to the ground, even a stirring in the air that perhaps she caused as she breathed. Then would come long stretches of total silence, and I would begin to fear that she had lost the way. At last after one interminably prolonged period of such silence I chose to strum my lyre again—its sudden sound, breaking into that murky quietude, was almost frightening even to me—and in relief I heard what must surely have been the quick intake of Eurydice's breath.

Thus I guided her upward by the sounds of my lyre, through dark, steep passages that I scarcely had noticed during my descent, but which now were challenging and difficult as I went the other way. It is easy enough to descend into Hell, for its gates will open readily for anyone; but climbing back up again into the light, ah, that is not so simple! I pressed on, scrambling and clambering over the slippery rocks, and strained my ears to hear the sound of Eurydice behind me, and from time to time I thought I did. But was it so, or only the invention of my eager mind? And why, as I drew ever closer to the gateway that would lead us out into the world again, did I no longer hear anything that might betoken her presence?

I turned a sharp bend in the passageway and I saw the light of the upper world gleaming just ahead of me. And in that critical moment I became possessed of the belief that Eurydice had strayed into some side passage and become lost. Despite Hades' terrible warning I turned, helpless to do otherwise, to reassure myself. And there she was.

But I had only the merest hasty glimpse of her, and she of me. For an instant I beheld her pale frightened face and her eyes wide with shock and horror at my transgression. And then the grinning shadowy minions of Hades came gliding out of the darkness to cluster about her and pluck at her with their talons.

"Oh, Orpheus—Orpheus—farewell forever!" she cried, in a faint, vanishing voice. Desperately she stretched her arms to me, and I toward her. But we could not so much as touch. And then, as they pulled her back from me, she became incorporeal and ghostly, a shadow of the woman that once had been, the merest of misty shades. I lunged for her and my arms closed on empty air. I beheld only a fleeting reproachful vision moving swiftly backward, fading from me like a wisp of smoke, and in another moment she had disappeared into the darkness and all I could hear was the eerie whistling sound as those merciless phantoms hurried her away from me to return her to Hades' kingdom.

So Eurydice met her second death, and my soul was devastated as it had not been even at the time of her first death, and I stood there frozen, dazed, knowing beyond all doubt that I had lost her forever.

8

eight

YOU ASK ME, then, why did I turn back to look at her, I who knew that Hades had explictly forbade it, I who can see all things past and future and who understood what the consequences of that single glance would be?

And I answer you that we are none of us allowed the option of deviating from the track that has been laid down for us by the gods. I *had* to turn back for that fatal glance, just as Oedipus had to slay the old man he encountered at the crossroads and thereby set in motion the relentless machinery that the gods had devised for him, and Agamemnon the lord of men had to bring his mistress Cassandra back from Troy with him and thus invite the wrath of his murderous wife Clytemnestra, and Jason of the *Argo* similarly to bring upon himself the bloody vengeance of the witch Medea, the mother of his sons, by spurning her for the Corinthian princess Creusa after his return from his great quest for the Fleece. The gods choose our destinies for us, and once we are set in our paths no foreknowledge of consequences can turn us for long from our dooms, not even I, who travel ceaselessly on the ever-repeating current that is my life.

And so I paused there at the brink of the upper world, with Eurydice's freedom all but achieved, and, caught in the toils of my destiny, I glanced helplessly back despite everything I knew would ensue, to see if she still followed me. Thus I lost her for all time, until the next return of existence, when I am fated to win and then to lose her again.

Even then there was more to my torment, much more. One is tempered in the fires of the gods; and because they had much need of me, they saw to it that my tempering was a thorough one.

Though I had no shred of hope it was necessary all the same for me to descend once more into Hell and follow that dank winding path to the Styx to confront stern Charon at his ferry station. "Take me across once again," I said to him, knowing what the reply would be. If there had been any laughter in his soul, I think he would have laughed at me, but all he did was stare in that icy way of his and shake his head.

It was pointless to try to charm him with my music, as I had done the last time. There was no music left in me then, and this time, even if there had been, he would have been armored against its powers. I asked, and he stared his refusal, and I asked again and he stared again, and once more I asked, and again he was silent. Then a pale shrouded wraith

appeared, a new dead soul making his pilgrimage to the kingdom within, and he stepped through me as though I were not
there and boarded Charon's boat, and the two of them glided
off into the darkness on the breast of that dread river, leaving
me alone on the bank.

Charon did not return. After a time I set out yet again on
the ascent to the land of the living.

Seven days and seven nights I lingered despondent at
Tainaron gate, unable either to go forward into the light or
to make yet another attempt at the darkness below. I went
without food or drink, and my lyre lay before me, untouched,
like a dead thing. When finally I picked it up again the first
sounds that came from it were hellish jangling ones, a dis-
sonant cacophony, which I could not master for several days
more. When finally I could play again I was able to sing only
a single bitter complaining song, over and over, until the
rocks about me themselves seemed bored with my constant
repetitive lament.

In time some vestige of life entered me again and I rose
and moved on. To Egypt then I went, where I hoped to escape
the agony of my grief over the second death of my beloved
under the scorching sun of that ancient land. I had never
known such despair before, because I had never known the
loss of love, since I had never known love itself. All that was
new to me, I who had never experienced anything for the first
time, for my love for Eurydice was an aspect of the mortal part
of myself, which does not see things the way the divine part
does. The pain of her double death wrapped itself about me
like a cloak of ice. I could not free myself from it, not even
with my own songs, that were able to charm the trees and the

rivers and the inanimate rocks; but it seemed to me that if I ran far enough and quickly enough, I might be able to escape even the inescapable and leave that great sadness behind.

And so, Egypt. At Pharaoh's court I dwelled, and there, under that cloudless sky, beside that broad reeking river, in that land of nightmare gods and many-columned temples as big as cities, I learned the magic of their priests and was initiated into the secrets of their beliefs and slowly, very slowly, began to enclose the running sore that was my great grief within an insulating shell of stone within my heart.

The *strangeness* of Egypt! How astounded I was by it!

As I have already told you, I was never young, as the world understands the ordinary meaning of that word. I came into the world ten thousand years old, and there is nothing that I can say I have seen for the first time, but, even so, though always I look backward and forward along the river of time, there was much that was new and strange to me in Egypt. Do I seem to contradict myself? Yes, I do; but I embody in myself all the contradictory things that men have believed of me. I confirm nothing; I deny nothing. I am Orpheus the demigod, and you must be a demigod to comprehend what that is like to be. I will help you as much as I can; but it will not be enough.

Egypt, then.

That blazing sun, that all-seeing fiery eye filling the heavens. The scent of unknown spices and the heavy reek of the enormous river. The carvings on the walls, the gods with the heads of hawks and vultures and lions; the snakes with legs; the beetles that spoke. The vast temples that were like forests of stone columns. The people with sly faces, moving busily but silently through the city streets, smiling, covertly staring at one another. Here and there I saw a swarthy bearded man who plainly was of Crete or Mycenae, or one from Babylon, or a little knot of black-skinned folk in robes as bright as the sun, for this was the great cosmopolitan center of the world. No one took notice of me. Why should they? I was cloaked in my grief and it made me invisible.

I went to the stone palace of their king and sang myself past its myriad guards into its airy halls.

Their king is called Pharaoh. So it has been for thousands of years. This Pharaoh was a small slender hawk-faced man, dark as ivory that has spent a century in the sun and almost fleshless, who wore a white cotton wrap around his loins and a lofty double crown, one part of it red and the other white, and a jewelled pendant on his bare breast, a heavy thing of gold and emeralds and rubies, that was so bright it hurt one's eyes to look upon it. He held a golden scepter in each hand, one that had the shape of a flail and one that had the shape of a crook, and he wore a stiff little false beard strapped to his chin.

"Well?" he said, and I struck a chord on my lyre and sang to him of the lands beyond Egypt that he had never known, king though he was of the mightiest of realms.

I sang to him of Hellas, its great jagged mountains and green plains and cool swift rivers, and of the islands about it in the sea that sparkled in the sunlight like his pendant. I sang of Troy, and of the war that had not happened yet, but would. I sang him Agamemnon and Clytemnestra; I sang him invincible Achilles and valiant Hector; I sang him Helen and Paris and Menelaus; I sang him Heracles and Icarus and Perseus, Theseus and Prometheus and King Oedipus. I sang him Zeus

and Apollo and Poseidon and Dionysus. Then I sang to him
of the mysterious humid jungles of Africa and the giant predatory beasts that prowl their vine-entangled paths. I sang of
the Hyperborean lands that I would visit in a later year, that
time when I would sail with Odysseus, those dark water-girt
lands, densely forested and green with rain, where the people
are as tall as this Pharaoh is short and as fair and golden as he
is dusky, and the summer days never end and cold thick snow
falls from the bleak gray sky in the wintry time of little light. I
sang of the far lands I have seen in dreams, where the yellow-
skinned shaven-headed emperors dine with sticks of ivory on
vessels of bronze and clothe their daughters in garments of
silk. I sang to him of mighty Rome that is yet to come, and
of the even mightier empires that will come still farther on in
time, in a day when men will fly through the air and journey
to other worlds. I even sang to him of those other worlds. I had
never sung so long nor so well in all my days. But I was not so
much singing for him as I was for myself, for I needed to sing
my way into Egypt in order to heal myself of my sorrow, and
as I sang I knew I was conquering him and would thus in time
conquer even my own intense and nearly unconsolable grief.

He listened without a word, gripping the sides of his golden
throne so hard his arms began to tremble. When I stopped he
pointed at my lyre with the flail-scepter and said, "What is
that thing? How is it made?"

"It is made of a frame and a sounding-board and strings,"
I said.

He beckoned with the scepter and I put the lyre in his
hands and he swept his fingers across the strings and made an
ugly discordant sound.

"No," I said. "Like this." I took it from him and sang him the first song of Orpheus and Eurydice, the happy one, the song of meeting and loving, and he began to weep. Great glossy tears ran down his fleshless face and vanished into the coarse bristles of that false beard. He seemed bewildered, as though he had never wept before: I think that was so. For he was a man of stone, if he was a man at all, this Pharaoh of Egypt. He was not accustomed to weeping. He maintained a godlike facade, and I think he believed, much of the time, in the reality of his own divinity, though behind that facade there was, I suppose, a real man, with all the doubts and fears and turmoils that real men have. Only through my music could I reach past the stony facade to the man within.

"Sing another," he said.

So I sang him the second song of Orpheus and Eurydice, the song of her death, and he wept again, though it was a different sort of weeping and it bewildered him even more. I sang him the song of my finding her. I sang him the song of my losing her again. Then he had had enough; the experience of feeling strong emotion was something new to him, I knew, and my singing brought him pain along with delight.

"You will make such instruments of music for us," said Pharaoh. "You will teach us the art."

I pressed my hand to my breast in acknowledgment of the command.

9

nine

PHARAOH GREW FOND of me. I became a
member of his court, the familiar of his high priests
and viziers. Each night when the furious sun dropped into the
western desert I sang before his throne, never the same song
twice. They all came to hear me. I made them weep; I made
them tremble. Music was not unknown to them, but they had
not known music like mine.

Proudly Pharaoh showed me his wives, some of whom, he
told me, were his sisters. The king here always marries his sisters. Well, Hera is the sister of Zeus, and the Egyptian goddess
Isis is the sister of their Osiris; evidently such marriages are
essential on the highest levels of the cosmos, and the kings
here imitate what the gods do, for they fancy that they are

gods themselves. He showed me the royal treasury, overflowing with the spoils of the nations. He allowed me to visit his great library, a lofty stone chamber full of paper scrolls that he said contained all the wisdom of the universe, though he did not allow me to look into them, not just yet. And he took me to see his tomb, which had been in the making for all the twenty years of his reign. A stone chamber, it was, on the far side of the great river that splits his land in two, or rather a whole series of chambers, descending deep into the earth so that he would sleep beyond the reach of the heat of the day when the time for him to sleep arrived. About it were many other such tombs, belonging to the earlier kings of his race.

On the walls of his tomb were paintings, bright and wondrous, showing the gods of his people and the judging of the dead, Pharaoh himself standing before them to offer an account of his life and his reign. A strange god with a brawny body and a bird's head weighed the heart of the king in a balance while the presiding god looked on, judging its merit. These gods, he said, are called Thoth and Osiris. The Egyptians have a multitude of gods, whom they call by Egyptian names, though of course all gods are the same, no matter what mortals may call them, certain names for the Egyptians and certain ones for the Babylonians and different ones for the people of the yellow lands: names are only names, but the gods are the same, be they Amon and Thoth or Zeus and Hermes, the patterns are the same everywhere: Osiris is a god who is slain and resurrected, and is that not true of Dionysus as well? Thoth is Hermes; Amon is not unlike far-seeing Zeus. And in the end all of them, Poseidon and Hermes and Dionysus and Ares and Athena, Horus and Osiris and Isis and Set, must be understood as mere aspects of the One God who rules the universe. I did not discuss these matters with Pharaoh, though later I would with his priests. What I did speak of with him was the art of music, and the methods by which his tomb had been carved into the rock, and when he showed me the colossal pyramidal mountains of stone that his distant ancestors had built as their own tombs at a time when such huge funerary monuments were in fashion, he explained to me the secret of how those tremendous blocks of granite had been trundled toward the site and lifted into position, telling me of the amazing levers and hoists and engines by which the job was done. But we did not ever discuss the nature of the gods.

I stayed in Egypt five years, or perhaps it was ten. The days went by quickly and under that implacable sun my sadness began gradually to melt. I showed them how to make lyres from a tortoise shell and a sounding-skin, and how to attach the strings and how to affix the decorative horns. Pharaoh complained that these lyres were not like my own, and I explained that a god had fashioned mine out of gold and it was the only one of its kind in the world. "Which god?" he demanded, and I hesitated a moment and said, "Thoth," for he knew nothing of Hermes. Since Thoth is the weigher of the souls of the dead the king did not care to have me invoke him, so nothing more was said about the making of a second lyre the equal of my own. But I could tell that he was displeased.

I taught his courtiers how to play the lyres that I made and how to sing to them, and they sang well enough, in their way, though there was no magic in their singing. How could there have been? I am Orpheus, who was made by the gods to bring music to this world of ours, and they were only men and women of the court of Pharaoh, constrained by all the constraints that hold the court of Pharaoh in an iron grip. For they do everything at the court of Pharaoh as it was done a thousand years before, and three thousand, and ten thousand. Nothing must change, they think, or the skies will fall. So they sing the melodies of Orpheus but they sing them in their rigid Egyptian way, stiff and jangling where my melodies are sinuous and gentle, and so everything is quite different. But they were happy with what they achieved and music resounded day and night in the halls of the palace of Pharaoh.

They are an interesting people. They have poetry and literature and painting, and do it all quite well. They have a kind of writing, too, a funny picture-writing, using images of snakes and beetles and owls and whips to stand for sounds and ideas, very cumbersome. I have devised a better system for my own people. I offered it to Pharaoh, but he would not have it: the more fool he, but Egypt's welfare is not my concern. Anyway, they are happy with the things they have, which will serve them for a very long time. But my kind of writing will outlast even theirs. A time will come when no one in the world will be able to read their writing, and it will be understood again only because men will find a text that has the same inscription in their writing and mine, which will still be capable of being read, so that they can compare and decipher the mysteries of those owl-pictures and beetle-pictures and summon sense and meaning from them again.

On the other hand, they have devoted many thousands of years to the study of the secrets of the soul, and have deep insight into such things. I learned all that I could of their magic. I learned of the Amulet of the Eye of Horus and the

Amulet of the Two Fingers and the Amulet of the Collar of Gold. I learned of the Seven Cows and the Four Rudders, and of the Gift of Air and Water. I learned the names of the Seven Gates and the words of the Coming Forth by Day. And when the great priest of Pharaoh offered to initiate me into the most sacred mysteries of Egypt, I accepted gladly: I have never been too proud to learn when learning is offered me. (I am like far-questing Odysseus in this. Of all mortal mankind there has never been anyone I admired more than clever Odysseus. I had no love for him, because he allowed his men to sack my city of Ismarus when they passed the coast of Thrace at the beginning of their journey home from Troy, but it was impossible not to admire the workings of his mind, and we would become friends, after a sort, long afterward.)

The Mysteries of Egypt were worthy mysteries, though they were not sufficient to the task, since they did not deal fully, as our Mysteries do, with the problems of creation and existence and death, though they do touch on the great matter of rebirth. Still, for all their gaps, they are excellent mysteries, full of truth. These Egyptian Mysteries I will not sing to you, Musaeus, not here, at any rate, because they are Mysteries sacred to those people and may not be treated that way, but you know something of them already. You know that they deal primarily with the fate of the soul after death. You know that they teach us that when breath leaves us we go before the judges of Hades and are consigned to our next existence according to our deserts, punishment for the wicked, happiness for the good. And then we drink the waters of Lethe and forget who we have been and are made ready for our new lives, and enter again a mortal body and are born once more, and the circle is complete, though at last a time comes, when one has undergone the full initiation, that final release from the body is granted.

So it is, at least, among mortals. For us who are not entirely mortal it is different, a cycle of eternal return, a dying and a coming to life again, even as the cornfield and the grapevine spring to new green growth after the brown barren time of winter has passed. I often wonder what it is like to be truly mortal, to be ordinary, to be not in the least mythical: to live only a short while, sixty or seventy years, and then to die and be forgotten, even by one's own sons, who are just like oneself and will quickly grow old and die in their turn. And when mortals return to life, as the Mysteries say they will, it is without memory of what they have been before, so that they must learn and do and suffer all over again. I have sired mortal children, Musaeus, many of them, your brothers and sisters, though you never knew them. Now and then I encounter them in the world, aging wrinkled people with thinning hair and sagging frames. Some of them are unable even to sing. It is all very strange.

I returned to the Mysteries into which the Egyptian priests initiated me, the Lesser Mysteries and the Greater Mysteries, until I had mastered them. Now that I was an initiate I wore clean white linen robes every day and dined only on greens and cheese, for I could touch neither meat nor wine except at the time of the sacrifices to the gods. All the ancient strangenesses of Egypt were piped into my eager mind, holy secrets that have guided me ever since, and which I impart, sparingly and with caution, to those I think merit knowing of them. In the temples of Egypt I learned all that there was to learn of the

struggle that awaits one when life has ended, of the judging of
the soul after death and of the soul's strange midnight wanderings through the twelve caverns of the Netherworld, surrounded on all sides by dread enemies that must be repulsed,
and of the lake of fire, and of the boat that sails the waters
beneath the world, and of the bull with four horns, and of
the Great One kneeling in the sacred barge, and much, much
more of which I may not speak. And although I had been to
the Netherworld myself, not once but many times in the eternal cycle that is my life, I came to understand much about it
from these priests that had not been clear to me before.

And then I knew that it was time for me to leave Egypt; for
I always know when it is time to close one phase of my journey
and begin the next. So I moved along from that sun-gripped
land and set forth to return to my native Thrace.

There I found my father Oeagros dying. He had just enough
strength left to speak of making a final journey into the wild
mountains of the north, as he had always said he would do
when he felt his end approaching, a journey from which there
would be no coming back. I offered him the consolations I had
learned in Egypt, but he would have none of them. In our land
Dionysus was the reigning god, the old fierce Dionysus whom
they worshipped with wild torch-bearing processions and the
drinking of wine and the rending of beasts and the guzzling
of their blood, and so my father ended his days with what he
saw as the proper homage to his god, making a last offering
to Dionysus, eating of the flesh and drinking of the blood,
and went on his solitary journey into the dark mountainous
wilderness dense with mighty trees that surrounded our city,
and that was the last of him. So for a time I ruled as king in

his place. Knowing that this was what I was meant to do at this point in my days I dwelled placidly among the roughhewn Ciconians and was for a time their ruler, their lawgiver, their teacher. I gave them the art of letters and showed them better ways of sowing their crops and made songs for them that tempered to some degree their cruel and savage spirits, and attempted to inculcate in them some of the true Mysteries, though that was hard, because I wanted to guide them toward the cool and disciplined way of Apollo and it was plain that they preferred the riotous and bloody way of Dionysus. I did my best. The years went by, and still I tarried in the land of the Ciconians. I lived there as king and lawgiver until Cheiron the king of the centaurs came to me and and stood looming above me with his great beard flowing down over the vast barrel of his horse-chest, and said I must sail with Jason, whose foster-father he was, on his quest for the Golden Fleece.

"Must I?" I said. "What good will be served by that? I am of great use doing what I do here."

Of course I knew in my heart that it is a waste of breath to question what has been determined for us by the gods. The voyage I would make with Jason would be an arduous and painful one, and plainly it was meant to be the next stage in my tempering; therefore it was mere folly to protest. But I had ruled long enough in Thrace to have come to cherish my role as teacher and counsellor, and it was my first response to balk at giving all that up merely to go off on some wild venture with a great fool like Jason.

But Cheiron, that noble creature with the head and shoulders and brawny chest of a god rising from the body of a magnificent horse, was the wisest of all his race, himself a master of the arts of medicine and music and gifted with the skill of prophecy, and he was patient with me. "You must go because you must go," he said simply, knowing that I would understand what he meant by that; but also he said, "Without you and your music, Orpheus, the voyage will not succeed, and the voyage must succeed, and therefore you must go."

That I had no choice in the matter was already clear to me, for one never has any choice in any matter; that there might be any merit in this quest of Jason's was something that could well be doubted, but it is madness to attempt to understand the reasons the gods have for what they decree; and that Zeus had sent the command to me by no less a messenger than Cheiron, the wise centaur king, told me that there must be some necessity underlying what one might easily regard as an idle and even wicked enterprise.

So I gave a great feast in honor of the noble centaur, and he and I sat up far into the night discussing high and serious matters, the subjects I had already devoted much of my life to contemplating: the nature of the gods, most particularly Apollo, who was as close to his heart as he was to mine, and the relationship of music to number, and the role of music in sustaining the movements of the stars, and the methods by which the dead can sometimes be restored to life, and many another subject; and in the morning I bade him farewell and began my preparations for joining Jason and his Argonauts. Which is how it happened that I went off with them to distant Colchis in quest of the Golden Fleece, and achieved much but suffered greatly in the course of those high deeds.

10

(en)

ABOUT THIS JASON—A brave man, but, as I
have said, a great fool—and this voyage to steal the
Golden Fleece, I will tell you many things, but first you must
know this:

In Thessaly in ancient times lived King Athamas, the son
of Aeolus, with his queen, Nephele. They had two children,
the boy Phrixus and the girl Helle. King Athamas in time put
aside his wife and took another, and Nephele feared that her
children might be in danger, for their stepmother did not love
them. She prayed to Hermes, who sent her a ram with golden
fleece; Nephele placed the children on that ram's back and it
vaulted into the sky, heading eastward across the strait that
divides Europe and Asia. In mid-flight Helle lost her grip and

tumbled into the sea, which is why that strait is called the Hellespont, but Phrixus held tight and was safely delivered to the land of Colchis far away on the eastern shore of the great body of water we call the Euxine Sea, which later men will know by the unkinder name of the Black Sea.

AIETES, king of Colchis, welcomed Phrixus, for he was under the command of Hermes to be hospitable to him, and gave him sanctuary. The ram who had borne him there was sacrificed as a thanksgiving-offering to Zeus; Phrixus gave its golden fleece to Aietes as the bride-price for the king's daughter Chalciope, and the fleece was placed in a consecrated grove, where it was guarded by a great serpent that slept neither by night nor day. But Aietes felt resentful that the gods had thrust Phrixus upon him, and when after a time Phrixus died, the king denied him a proper burial of the sort practiced in all the Hellene lands. In Colchis it is the strange custom that only women are given burial; the bodies of men are wrapped in ox-hides and they hang them up exposed in trees for the birds to eat, and that was what was done with the body of Phrixus. Because of that the ghost of Phrixus was compelled to wander disconsolately about in Colchis with no way to attain proper rest. This is the story as it was told to me; whether it is true or not, I cannot say. You already know of me that I neither confirm nor deny.

Now to sing of Jason: like Phrixus a man of Thessaly and indeed his kinsman, Jason was the son of Aeson, who ruled the kingdom of Iolcus, close beside the land where Athamas, the father of Phrixus, was king; and Aeson was a son of Cretheus, brother of Athamas, so Aeson and Phrixus were cousins. Jason's name at birth was Diomedes. King Aeson was a mild and gentle man, but his warlike half-brother Pelias, coveting the throne, forced him to yield his crown to him when Aeson's son Diomedes was only a babe, though Pelias promised that when Diomedes reached manhood he would surrender the royal power to him. Aeson was kept a prisoner thereafter in Pelias' palace; as for Diomedes, a kindly servant saw to it that he was smuggled out of Iolcus to Mount Pelion, where he was placed in the care of the centaur Cheiron. The centaur gave him the new name of Jason, meaning "healer," and raised him there until he was grown. This much I know to be true, for Cheiron told me so himself.

The usurper Pelias, ruling unchallenged in Iolcus, was haunted by the ghost of his cousin Phrixus, who told him in dreams that neither Pelias nor any of his kin would flourish until both Phrixus and the fleece of the golden ram that had carried him to Colchis were brought back to Thessaly. Pelias also was troubled by an oracle's tale that a man with one sandal would come to his city and overthrow him. And indeed one day a man with one foot bare did arrive in Iolcus: none other than Jason, now full-grown and intending to restore his father to the throne. He had lost the sandal while helping the goddess Hera, in the guise of an old woman, to cross a river, and by so doing had won the gratitude and the protection of the queen of the gods.

Jason was taken before Pelias, and boldly—or, one might say, foolishly—told him that the name he bore was one that his foster-father Cheiron had given him, but before he was Jason he had been Diomedes, son of King Aeson. He demanded that Pelias step down from the throne, as he had sworn to do long ago; and the deceitful Pelias, pretending great love for his brother and his brother's son, replied without hesitation that he would, but on one condition.

"And what may that be?" asked Jason.

"This land is under the curse of our kinsman Phrixus, whose spirit wanders unhallowed in Colchis. An oracle has told me that there will be no peace for our family until he is returned to the city of his birth, and that must be done only in a certain way. Therefore build a ship and sail to Colchis, and bring the ghost of Phrixus home to Iolcus aboard that ship, and bring with it the fleece of the golden ram that had carried him as a fugitive to Colchis before you were born."

That seemed to Pelias the perfect way to rid himself of Jason; for the sea voyage to Colchis was so fraught with perils that it was almost impossible to survive, and in any event stealing the Golden Fleece from under the baleful glare of that unsleeping dragon was something that no one could achieve. But Jason, as I have said twice now, was a great fool, though a brave man, and he set out forthwith to build the ship and bring Phrixus and the fleece home from Colchis.

Whereupon Cheiron the centaur came to me in Thrace and told me that I was essential to the success of Jason's voyage, and I yielded to the inevitability of the gods' decree, and so my involvement with Jason and his Argonauts began.

"Argonauts," we were called, because the name of our craft was *Argo*, and that in honor of Argus of Thespiae, who with the help of Athena built that great vessel at Pagasae on the Magnesian coast in Thessaly just east of Iolcus. It was a splendid ship. None so grand had ever been built before, and not until long after our times would its equal be seen on the seas. A well-balanced fifty-oared galley, it was, slender and graceful, built for speed, with a keel and frame of oak and planks of pine brought from the forested slopes of Mount Pelion, all of them fastened in place with bronze nails and caulked with tar. A sturdy mast of fir that would soar far over our heads was nearing completion when I arrived at Pasagae. The bottom had already been finished and the close-set ribs were rising, but I watched that great shipwright put in the long side-planking and construct the half-decks, and fence the hull about with a latticed bulwark to keep the water out, and build a broad oar to steer her with, and fashion a wondrous square sail out of the white linen cloth of Egypt to cling to that mighty mast. For her prow Argus took a great beam from the roof of the royal palace in Iolcus that had come from Zeus' sacred grove in Dodona.

The sound of hammering went on day and night. The magnificent vessel, with timbers painted blue and gold and crimson, came rapidly toward completion; and meanwhile the band of heroes who would take her to Colchis was assembling, summoned from far and wide at Jason's behest.

Such a group of voyagers had never been brought together before. Heracles himself was among us, that giant among men, and Peleus, the father of Achilles, and Odysseus' father Laertes. A phalanx of sons of trident-wielding Poseidon would be aboard: Ancaeus of Tegea, Erginus of Miletus, Melampus of Pylos, Nauplius of Argos. It is always good to have sons of Poseidon among one's shipmates, for the sea-god will look after them and their companions. Nor were the other Olympian gods unrepresented, for also we had bronze-helmed Ares' son Ascalaphus of Orchomenus, Hermes' son Echion of Mount Cyllene and also his guileful brother Erytus, and Idmon the Argive, Apollo's son. Heracles, as everyone knows, was begotten by Father Zeus, and with us as well were two more of Zeus's get, Castor of Sparta and his brother, the invincible boxer Polydeuces. Then there were winged Zetes and Calais, the sons of the north wind Boreas. We would have had famed Theseus with us too, another hero of Poseidon's making, but a different task detained him at the time. You will find in the writings of the poets who wrote of our journey in the years afterward the names of many others also, hundreds of them all told, who are said to have sailed aboard the *Argo*, for every city has its poet and what city would not have wanted to claim its share of that fabled voyage? But I assure you that our ship had but fifty oars. I will not list all the others who actually did go with us: suffice it to say it was an extraordinary gathering of men, and even one woman, Atalanta the long-legged virgin huntress, whose beauty and swiftness of foot impelled Jason to include her in our group.

It will not surprise you to hear that such a band of proud heroes might be inclined toward quarrelsomeness, especially when wine had been flowing quickly; and so, very shortly, it was made clear to me why the gods had chosen me to accompany them. For only through the calming influence of song could these headstrong and boisterous men be made to remain at peace with one another.

They were fighting among themselves on the beach at Pagasae when I first came among them. Our captain Jason, for all his strength and valor, and he was richly endowed with both, was a brooding indecisive man. He had been lost in some somber meditation on the wisdom of undertaking the voyage when Idas of Messene drunkenly accused him of cowardice, and then loudly bragged that even if all-seeing Zeus himself sent misfortune to the *Argo*, Idas would fend it off. Idmon, who was one who laid claim to having been engendered by Apollo, took offense at this boastfulness, and berated Idas for it, as did Polydeuces the boxer, who knocked Idas down when Idas angrily brandished his spear. Then Lynceus, the brother of Idas, came running up, sword in hand, to take his brother's part, and chaos and bloodshed threatened.

It was at this moment that I made my appearance in their midst. Brooding, anguished Jason caught me by the wrist and said, "Orpheus! By the gods, you come to us at a welcome time! You who can lure oak trees out of the forest and down to the seashore by the sound of your lyre, quickly play a melody that will soothe these madmen before we are all lost."

So that is what he thought, that I have lured oak trees from the forest to the seashore with my music? Well, people think many things of me. I do not confirm them; neither will I deny them. But most assuredly I know the art of calming angry men. So I unslung my lyre and whacked its sounding-board with my hand to get their attention, and struck a chord or two, and began to sing the first song that came to my lips.

What I sang was the song of the Creation, the song of that time before time when there was neither light nor darkness, but only the primordial dimness, and sky and earth and sea all were one. I sang of how they struggled mightily among themselves, each yearning to escape the others' grip, until a forceful music arose out of the heart of the universe and they were sundered by it. I sang of the stars in the heavens, and how they travel their appointed courses, each making its own sweet sound as it moves, thereby bringing forth wonderful music as they sail above us, the great song of the cosmos. I sang of the primordial oneness of water and earth, out of which came Phanes, the creator of all, from whom the cosmos had its first origin. I told of how Phanes made the sun and the moon, and the first men, too, who were not of our race, and have long since vanished from the world. I sang then of how Phanes brought forth a daughter, Night, to whom he handed the supreme power when he grew weary of wielding it, and from whom came Gaia and Uranus, the earth and the heaven. From them, I told, came the race of Titans, Cronos, Rhea, and all the rest; and then I sang of how Cronos overthrew his father Uranus, and by Rhea brought forth the next generation of gods, Zeus and his brothers and sisters, and how there was increasing dissension among them until the cosmos was on the verge of degenerating into discord, until Zeus of the lightning-bolts came forth to overthrow his royal father Cronos and take his place atop snowy Olympus and bring the world under his wise rule. And at last I sang of the swallowing of the world-creator Phanes by Zeus, so that he would encompass all things within himself, both the beginning and the end, and could create all things anew, including the race of men that endures today. I might have sung some other version of the tale entirely, and then a different one from that, for there are many such stories of the succession of the eras of the gods, and no two of them are the same, but all of them are true. The one I sang was the proper one for that occasion. By the time I had reached the point in my song that told of the setting aside of

Cronos by Zeus, the restoration of order in the world, and the engulfing of Phanes, the Argonauts had recovered from their fit of madness. The swords were sheathed, the spears were laid aside, and they were dancing drunkenly on the beach, even Jason capering nimbly, his arms over his head, his fingers snapping. And that was the end of it; but I had served my purpose. It would not be the last such time.

11

eleven

WE BUILT THE rollers and fastened the ropes and hoisted the *Argo* to its track and hauled it down to the shore, putting our backs to it and straining to keep her moving forward. Smoke, dark and bitter-smelling, rose from the rollers under the weight of that mighty keel. I will not pretend it was anything but a horrendous struggle to get that ship to the sea. You will hear poets say that with a few chords of my lyre I magicked the vessel into gliding down to the water of her own accord, and it is, as I have made clear, my custom with these tales neither to confirm or deny; but if you are willing to believe that, you will believe anything. Soon enough, at any rate, the *Argo* approached the sea's edge and we launched it into the gulf and set the mast and raised the sail; and our voyage to Colchis began.

It was at dawn we left, after sacrificing two robust oxen to Apollo, who presides over the embarkation of mariners. Tiphys of Siphae was our helmsman, a man exceedingly skilled in the ways of the winds and the stars and the signs by which a craft is steered, and he it was who took us eastward from Thessaly across the sea. The winds were contrary that day and we had to make our departure under the power of our oars alone. It was my task to beat time for the oarsmen with my lyre. I set them a good pace, for they were young men and vigorous ones, who sang to my music as they pulled, and the blades of their oars bit keenly into the foaming water. Each bench held two oarsmen, their places having been decided by lot—all but the place of Heracles, who because of his great size and overwhelming strength must of necessity sit amidships, since otherwise the great force of his giant oar would overbalance the vessel and make it difficult to hold her to a straight course. For his benchmate Jason gave him that massive man Ancaeus, one of the several among us who had sprung from the seed of the god Poseidon.

Soon a favorable wind came to us and we lifted the great mast into position and unfurled our broad sail of white linen from Egypt and tied its lines in place. It swelled in the breeze and we journeyed smoothly on beyond Mount Pelion, where the centaur Cheiron came down to the sea and waded out into the surf to wave to us. Cheiron was accompanied by his wife, the nymph Charicio. She carried in her arms their latest foster-child, Achilles, son of Peleus and the sea-nymph Thetis, and held the babe up so that his father might see him. The world would hear much more of Achilles in the generation to come.

We left the booming surf and the hissing combers behind and moved out into the open waters. I beat the time and the oarsmen pulled merrily at the oars and we sped along, though despite the strength and elegance of our smooth-sided vessel it was anything but easy work. The angry wind shrieked and roared overhead and the mainsail strained at its creaking ropes, and great waves loomed about us, mountain-high, crashing athwart our bow and sending fountains of cold white spume across our open deck. Now and again, as we headed farther out from shore, we moved through a cloud of low-hanging silvery mist so thick that we could barely see an oar's length in front of us, and as we surged upward on the breast of a soaring wave some great black fang of rock, glossy with sea-foam, would rise abruptly before us out of the heaving waters; but Tiphys our master helmsman was ever adroit, and used his wits to steer us clear of danger.

The wind carried us well, though. Soon we moved past headlands sacred to Artemis, and I sang a hymn to her as we went by. A stiff breeze took us swiftly under the shadow of great Mount Athos in Thrace, but at dawn we were becalmed once more, and it was by the strength of our oarsmen alone that we were able to journey on to the isle of Lemnos. The women of this island, angered by the faithlessness of their men, had fallen upon them one night and slaughtered every one of them; but now they had grown weary of life without a man's embrace, and when we appeared before them they turned to us with unseemly eagerness. Therefore, alas, we wasted much time on Lemnos because foolish Jason became entangled in a dalliance with the island's voluptuous queen, and many another of us, seeing our captain so entranced by love, behaved in similar fashion, though not I, because for me there could be no woman after Eurydice. It seemed as though we would remain there forever, lost in this lustful idleness; but at last the anger of Heracles awakened Jason from his dream and led him back to his task.

Thence we went to Samothrace, an island holy to Persephone. Here I felt it needful to pause and take part in the Mysteries that are practiced there in her honor, not only in regard for the aid that Hades' queen had offered me in my futile quest to regain Eurydice but also because I knew that my shipmates and I must do whatever we could to gain the love of the gods if we were to succeed in this perilous adventure.

So I clad myself in the white robe marked with a jagged streak of golden lightning that I had brought with me from Egypt and went ashore to meet with the priestess, who could tell immediately, from that robe, that I was an initiate. She agreed to my request, and I returned to the ship and gathered up ten of the Argonauts, those whom I felt would best be able to benefit from the rites in which they would take part. Jason was one of the ones I chose, but when the priestess saw him she hesitated, and seemed about to reject him from the group. Then she relented and let him stay, though plainly she perceived the great flaws in him that were beyond redemption and would lead eventually to his undoing.

I cannot, of course, sing of the Mysteries except in the most superficial way. Like all Mysteries, they tell of birth and life and death and resurrection. I can tell you that we acted out the rite of Creation first, building the circular mound of earth and surrounding it with a water-filled trench and dancing on it and saying the Words of Coming Forth, and then the serpent was brought out and the gong was sounded and the flutes played, and after that came the rite of the dove and the crab, and the ceremonies of Priapus. At last the acolytes, with faces and bodies powdered with gypsum so that they were snowy white, brought out the little bull-calf for the sacrifice, and shed its blood and sprinkled it on Jason and his companions, after which came the ritual ablution, and the rite of rebirth and the anointing with oil, and then the final rite whose very name cannot be spoken. The men were solemn and silent as we made our way back to the *Argo*, and I heard none of them speak of what they had witnessed that night, though I knew they had been profoundly shaken by it. In my solitude aforedeck I sang the songs of my love for Eurydice again, softly singing for myself alone, telling myself once more how I had won her and lost her and won her again by Persephone's favor, and had lost her the second time because that was the path that the gods had made a necessary part of the toilsome journey that is my life. Necessary, yes; but the pain of it will always be with me.

Our next landfall was along the coast of Mysia as we made our way northward and eastward toward the Hellespont strait that would admit us to the sea where Colchis lay. The wind had been slack for several days, but we were making good headway along that coast by the use of our oars alone, with the prodigious indefatigable Heracles setting an unmatchable pace. Only Jason was able to equal him for a time; and then even Jason fell forward over his oar and collapsed in exhaustion. At that same moment Heracles' mighty oar snapped in half from the force of his exertions. He glared at the stump of it in fury and disgust. We had no alternative but to put ashore to allow him to search out a tree from which he could make a new one.

We made camp on the shore. Within a couple of hours Heracles returned from the interior, dragging behind him a colossal fir tree that he set about trimming to shape. Meanwhile, though, Heracles' squire Hylas, had gone off toward a nearby pool to fetch water, and had not returned. This Hylas was a pretty young man whom Heracles, who had taken him as a lover, had insisted that we bring with us on the voyage. Jason had sent staunch Polyphemus the Arcadian, one of our most sober and reliable men, to find him, and he had not returned either.

After a while Heracles noticed that Hylas was not in the camp, and when someone told him where he had gone and how long he had been absent, Heracles went rushing off into the forest, frantically shouting his name. What happened after that I learned many years later, when I encountered Heracles in Thrace. In the forest he found only Polyphemus, who had been to the pool and discovered Hylas' water-pitcher lying abandoned beside it. Of Hylas himself there was no trace, and Polyphemus suggested that the pretty boy had been carried off by nymphs of the pool or forest who had taken a fancy to him. Heracles, with a great roar of rage, cried that they must search until they found him, and so they did, for when dawn came there was no sign in camp of either man, let alone the one for whom they had gone in search.

Meanwhile a fair breeze had sprung up at last, and to the astonishment of everyone Jason gave the order for us to resume the voyage. "But where is Heracles?" Admetus of Pherae asked, as we settled into our places aboard the *Argo*. "Where is Polyphemus?" Others—Peleus, Acastus—took up the cry. Jason, glowering, merely shrugged and said the gods wished us to be on our way, and that he was not going to offend them by waiting any longer for Heracles and Polyphemus. Nor did we, though there was a noisy quarrel first, Admetus claiming that Jason was marooning Heracles out of jealousy, because Heracles had humiliated him by rowing so vigorously that Jason had been outmanned at the oars. To this accusation Jason made no answer, but simply went about directing the raising of the mast and the hoisting of the sail. In the end Mopsus the Lapith, who had the powers of a soothsayer, ended the wrangling by going into a trance, or pretending to do so, and announcing that it was the will of Zeus that Heracles and Polyphemus be left behind, for great-thewed Heracles was so rash that he would endanger the expedition when it came to the land of the Golden Fleece, and Polyphemus was needed for some task in another place. So we went on, having lost the services of two of our most valuable shipmates.

We were to have yet another such unhappy landing farther along. In the land of the Doliones we were given a warm welcome by Cyzicus, their king, but when we took our leave a contrary gale seized hold of us in the night, swinging us about in the sea and sending wild waters spilling across our deck, and carrying us back all unawares to the harbor from which we had just set out; and Cyzicus, thinking his city was being attacked by pirates, led an armed force out against us as we came ashore. In the darkness and confusion we slew our former host and a great number of his stalwart men. I watched the carnage from one side, for I am not a warrior and the taking of life is not what the gods meant me to do; but I knew that this tragic error could not be prevented, and though I did not slay, neither did I do anything to intervene.

Afterward we held funeral games in Cyzicus' honor, and sacrificed many a beast in atonement for the bloodshed we had unwittingly brought about, but even so we were kept in harbor for twelve days by foul weather before we could at last depart from that sorry land. Great was my own regret that I could not have averted this sad mistake; but I knew that I had to let events unfold, for King Cyzicus, despite his kindness to us, had been marked for death by the goddess Rhea, whose sacred lion he had slain on Mount Dindymum. We are eternally caught up, mortals and demigods alike, in the larger patterns that the gods have decreed.

Nor did we bring great joy to our next port of call. The isle of Bebrycos was ruled by the savage King Amycus, who fancied himself a great boxer and would give us neither food nor water until one of our men fought a contest with him. We learned that Amycus invariably won these matches and put the loser to death, and that any voyagers who refused to meet his challenge were summarily flung over the side of a cliff into the sea. Well, we sent our gallant Polydeuces against him, he who had been the victor time and again in the Olympic Games, and although Amycus was as strong as a bull and a ferocious boxer besides, Polydeuces was more skillful and struck him such a blow that he fell down dead. This led us into a battle with the infuriated Bebryceans, and once again our swordsmen were forced to slay many of them in our own necessary defense. You who live after us will say that was a

cruel age, our age, and indeed it was: many good men fell in such needless quarrels, for when strife arose our heroes looked upon the shedding of blood as unavoidable. Since Amycus was said to be yet another son of Poseidon, we placated that god by sacrificing twenty red bulls to him that we found in the city, and put to sea the next day.

Now we were approaching the Hellespont. We had been warned that the watchful men of Troy maintained a close surveillance over its eastern shore and would attack any vessel that approached their territory, so we took the precaution of painting our handsome white sail with the black ink of cuttlefish ink, which royal Peleus had brought along to be used in flavoring our stews and porridges. It was a sad thing to expend that delectable stuff for such a purpose as this, but we feared that the Trojan watchmen would see the glint of moonlight on our bright sail as we passed by; and so we mixed the cuttlefish ink with water and painted our sail until it was an ugly muddy hue. And by such a deception we went safely past the vigilant guardians of the great city of Troy and entered into the Hellespont.

BEYOND that strait lay a second and larger strait, the Bosphorus, that narrow stretch of swift water that would carry us into the Euxine Sea. But legend had it that at the upper end of the Bosphorus the way was barred to navigators by the Clashing Rocks, two floating islands that constantly tossed and heaved. When—so it was said—any ship began to enter the passage, the rocks would come together as though they

had been endowed with malice, grinding and crushing the unfortunate craft that was passing between them. It was King Pelias' hope that that fate would befall the ship of Jason and his comrades and put an end to whatever threat Jason posed to his own reign; and so he had compelled Jason to take the sea route to Colchis, knowing it must inevitably send him through the Clashing Rocks.

Many of our Argonauts believed in miracles and never doubted that the *Argo* would safely reach Colchis or that the Golden Fleece would fall readily into Jason's hands, and they gave little thought to the difficulties that these rocks presented. "Can you charm them into holding still as we go past?" more than one of them asked me. I simply smiled. I know what power my music holds, but also I know what it cannot achieve, and there was no way that the sounds of my lyre could keep those huge rocks from bobbing as they wished on the breast of the tossing water. But Jason, for all his valor, was a brooding fearful man, and although he had forced himself not to think about the Clashing Rocks in the early days of our voyage, he quite openly began to wonder now what chance we had of surviving that fearful passage.

Our shrewd helmsman Tiphys, it was, who set his mind at rest. Pointing ahead along the coast of Thrace, he said calmly, "Before us lies Salmydessus, whose king is Phineus, the son of Agenor. He knows the secret of the rocks and will tell us how to get ourselves safely through their jaws."

That unhappy king's land lay on the western shore of the Bosphorus close by the water, not very far beyond the mouth of the Hellespont. It once had been a prosperous realm, and Phineus, aspiring to the wisdom of the gods, had

accordingly been endowed by Zeus with the gift of prophecy. But he had grievously misused it, widely and carelessly sharing the confidences that the Great Father offered him without tact or forethought, and in the end he was visited with an awful punishment. He had been allowed to live on into old age, but his sight and strength had been taken from him, and food had become devoid of all savor for him, so that he could eat next to nothing. One splendid dish after another would be placed before him, but after a nibble or two Phineus turned aside, shuddering and waving the food away, and therefore in the prime of his manhood he had become a feeble, shrunken, trembling yellowed thing, more dead than alive, tottering about with the aid of a gnarled crooked staff.

Phineus still was able to see into the future, though, and so he knew that the gods had ordained that relief from his torment would come when a sturdy black-sailed ship with blue and gold and crimson timbers, with fifty renowned heroes aboard, pulled into his harbor. He greeted us, therefore, with such joy and gladness as his withered body could muster, and we performed the rites necessary to purify him and cleanse him of his sin, and for the first time in many years he was able to taste his victuals without revulsion. In return he shared with us those secrets of the Bosphorus and the great sea behind it that we needed to know if we were to complete our voyage to Colchis. He was shrewd enough to know that he dared not tell us all that Zeus had in store for us on our voyage, having learned his lesson in that regard, but he could at least recompense us in some measure for the service we had performed for him.

"The Bosphorus," he told us, "is nearly twenty miles long from end to end, but in places is less than half a mile wide between its banks; and thus it is more like a swift river than like an ordinary strait. Above it lies the mighty Euxine Sea, five hundred miles broad and nearly a thousand miles long. Before you enter it, though, you must pass between the Clashing Rocks, and that is no easy matter. Indeed, no ship has ever succeeded."

"They are not a legend, then," said Jason soberly.

"Not a legend at all," Phineus replied. And he confirmed all that we had heard of those deadly rocks, telling us how they guarded the narrows at the upper end of the Bosphorus, indeed moving one against the other whenever the spirit moved them, grinding to splinters any vessel unfortunate enough to be between them when they came together.

But, he said, there was a way to outwit even such malign rocks as those. If we found them quiescent and apart as we approached them, that meant that they were lying in wait for some victim to present itself, holding themselves poised on the verge of their next movement toward each other. It was possible then to deceive them and keep them from the goal that they sought, the destruction of ships. As we lay before them we should send out a dove to go ahead of us. The bird would fly between the rocks and very likely the rocks would close upon it, out of their sheer noxious eagerness to do harm. If the gods favored it, the bird would safely negotiate the dire passage; or perhaps the poor creature would be caught and crushed. Either way, though, the rocks would withdraw for a time to restore their baneful energies before making their next inward approach, and in that span we must use all our energy to thrust ourselves between them and move on into the sea beyond.

And so it came to pass. We traveled up the swift Bosphorus, fighting against the eddies and counter-currents as the strait narrowed, and narrowed and narrowed again. More than once we felt sure we would be swept against the treacherous rocks that lined its shore, but the skill of Tiphys took us past every peril, with, I must say, some aid from me, for I beat the time in an ever-increasing pace to push our oarsmen to the greatest effort. And then at last we were beyond the worst of the currents and nothing more remained between us and the Euxine except the Clashing Rocks themselves, which we knew, from the way the dark water was surging and hissing and boiling before us, lay just ahead.

They were two craggy menacing fangs, towering high above the ship. But we tried to look upon them as no more than a pair of ordinary rocky masses, one to our left, the other to our right, with a clear space between them for our passage. We did not make the mistake of underestimating the danger that they posed, however, and we followed the advice of Phineus in every degree. We had with us aboard the *Argo* some caged doves trained to aid us in our navigation, and skillful Euphemus of Tainaron, our birdmaster, selected one and set it free. Up it soared, and went straightaway toward the opening between the two rocks.

At once there was a groaning sound as one sometimes hears at the outset of an earthquake, and the rocks began to move toward each other with frightening speed. It was a horrific thing to behold. Onward sped the dove, undaunted. Then, from nowhere, a hawk dropped down out of the sky and lunged toward it in an attempt to seize it in midair, but in that same moment quick-witted Phalerus the archer, of the royal house of Attica, seized his bow and put a shaft through the hawk's heart. The hawk fell to our deck; the dove continued on; the rocks crashed together with a deafening sound like that of ten thunderbolts at once, throwing up a great surge of spray and rocking our ship to one side and the other until we thought she would capsize; and as the rocks parted again and the agitated sea grew calmer, we caught sight of our dove winging onward toward the Euxine, while a single tail feather came drifting down and was lost in the sea.

We wasted no time. The rocks had moved back, but who knew for how long? I took up my lyre and began a hearty song that set the strongest of rhythms, Tiphys clung to his steering-oar with all his might, our oarsmen rowed so hard their oars were nearly bending in the water, and sturdy *Argo* went pressing forward. As we passed between the rocks we heard the groaning sound again, and the beginning of the thunder, and when I made so bold as to look behind me I saw the two great cliffs starting to move inward a second time. But the men rowed like demons and we went plunging forward and came safely through, though the rocks came clashing together just behind us with a sound like that of a herald announcing the end of the world. Just as our dove had lost one of her feathers, we lost a piece of our stern orna-ment when the rocks clashed for that second time, but we sustained no other harm.

SO we left the Bosphorus and its Clashing Rocks behind, and entered onto the bosom of that great sea at whose farther end lay Colchis and the Fleece. And the tale is told among men that the Clashing Rocks, now that they had been outwitted by the *Argo*, grew roots in the sea and never again moved from their places.

12

twelve

THE STORY OF our voyage up the Euxine Sea to Colchis is something everyone knows, for the tale has been told again and again by the poets. But the daily toil, the pain, the struggle—ah, who can know of that who was not there? For me the suffering was a required ordeal, part of the education that the gods had designed for me; what it signified for the others, I cannot say. But though we suffered greatly, we none of us uttered a word of complaint. Through suffering comes purification.

Day after day we followed along the edge of those great waters, a voyage such as few had ever made, day succeeding day, pink dawn and golden noon and red twilight and purple night, and dawn again and noon and night, and dawn again, and noon and twilight and night, and on and on we went on the breast of that arduous sea. There was salt in our lungs, the salt of the sea-breezes that we inhaled with every pull of the oars. The blazing sun baked our skins. The hard dry wind out of the east assailed our aching eyes. Along the shore tall cities flamed in the sun, stone buildings, gold-fretted temples, courses of white paving-stones leading down to the sea, bright in the blaze of the morning light. Rarely did we halt at any of them, but continued going ever deeper into the unknown, moving past the mysterious kingdoms of the Euxine that nestled in the blue valleys descending between the great round mist-wrapped hills.

The land of the Bithynians, Phineus had told us, lay on our right, but he warned us to make no landing there. We went past it and the mouth of the River Rhebas and the Black Cape and, with our provisions beginning now to run low, we made our first landfall on the little low-lying isle of Thynias to seek meat and fresh water. There Apollo appeared before me in all his divine splendor, golden hair streaming in the wind, his silver bow in his left hand and the ground atremble beneath his feet as he strode by, and I built an altar in his honor and sacrificed a wild goat to him, and pledged myself anew to his service.

Beyond there we traveled awhile without going ashore, but when we drew near the city of Mariandyne, King Lycus' land, Jason, feeling fretful and anxious and desirous of diversion and sport, ordered us to put the *Argo* into its harbor. It was an unlucky choice, one of many that our uneasy captain was destined to make.

There is at Mariandyne an entrance to the Netherworld that no one had ever entered and survived, though Heracles, some years hence, would go down into it and return—a frightful chasm through which the icy waters of the Acheron come bursting to the surface, coating the surrounding rocks with glittering frost. Perhaps it was the cold wind that endlessly blows there from below that brought us ill luck, for at Mariandyne we lost Idmon the Argive, a hot-tempered man but a tireless and valuable one. Idmon had some gift as a soothsayer, and had dreamed, the night before, a dream that seemed to foretell his death; but nevertheless he took part in a boar-hunt the next morning, and as he passed beside a reedy meadow a great white-tusked boar sprang up from the side of a stream and gored him in the thigh, so that a fountain of blood spurted from it. Peleus and Idas carried him back to the ship, but he died in their arms before they reached it.

Even while we were still mourning for Idmon we suffered an even more grievous loss, a true catastrophe. In the family of Tiphys the helmsman it was a tradition that no man could live longer than the age of nine and forty years, for there was a curse on his line: Tiphys' grandfather had been imprudent enough once to cut down a sacred oak, and forty-nine was the number of the years that that oak had lived before it was felled. Tiphys now had reached the same age, and had known from the start of the voyage that he would not survive it. In Mariandyne he fell ill and wasted quickly away, despite the efforts of those among us who understood the medicinal arts; for the most efficacious medicines in the world are helpless against the inescapable decrees that shape our fates.

So Tiphys the irreplaceable was lost, and it was our task to replace him. Jason looked to those sons of the sea-lord Poseidon who were in our midst, of course, Nauplius of Argos, Erginus of Miletus, Melampus of Pylos, and Ancaeus of Tegea, and for a time we debated their various merits among ourselves. In the end Jason gave the nod to Ancaeus, whose strength and courage in time of crisis were beyond debate. And indeed he served us well throughout the remainder of the voyage, though no man could ever have matched Tiphys in his guileful mastery of the sea. After twelve unhappy days in Mariandyne we took to the water once more.

THE wind was strong behind us and our oarsmen enjoyed a holiday as the breezes carried us along. To Sinope in Paphlagonia we went, where Jason recruited the brothers Deileon, Autolycus, and Phlogius to fill three of the empty seats on our benches, and then past the river called the Thermodon, that has only four branches short of a hundred, and amidst whose headlands the Amazon women are said to dwell, and after that to the land of the Chalybes, who dig iron from the ground and refine it in an everlasting cloud of black smoke to sell to neighboring tribes. Phineus had advised us to halt next at the Isle of Ares, which we found to be a place infested by huge swarms of such fierce predatory birds that we had to drive them off by pounding on our helmets and shouting with all our might. This we did, and the birds fled, but we wondered why Phineus had told us to put in at this inhospitable site. Soon we had our answer when we came upon four castaways, who said they were brothers, the sons of Phrixus, he who had been carried to Colchis on the back of the ram that bore the fleece of gold. They had been shipwrecked here, they said, while attempting to return from unfriendly Colchis to the land of their grandfather Athamas in distant Thessaly.

Jason, greatly surprised, let them know that he was the grandson of Athamas' brother Cretheus, and therefore he and they were cousins. He explained that we were even then en route to Colchis to bring home not only the Golden Fleece but the troubled wandering spirit of his uncle Phrixus, their father; and we took them aboard to swell our number.

Now our goal was within reach. Nightfall brought us to an island called Philyra, which had its name because the centaur Cheiron was engendered there long ago by Cronos, king of the Titans, deceiving his wife the goddess Rhea with Philyra, the daughter of Ocean. Cronos, surprised by Rhea in the very act, transformed himself into a stallion and went galloping away, leaving Philyra impregnated with a strange creature that took on half the form of the stallion itself. Or so the story goes. I have never asked Cheiron about the truth of it. At any rate, we passed Philyra and several countries upwater from it, traveling now at great speed before a friendly wind, and saw the lofty peaks of the Caucasus before us, where the Titan Prometheus was chained after his defiance of Zeus and suffers the eternal torment of having an eagle gnaw at his liver, and then the Euxine came to its end.

In front of us now was the mouth of the broad swift-flowing river called the Phasis, which is the river that waters Colchis. We wept with joy, knowing that our quest was nearly done. Jason poured out a libation of wine and honey in gratitude to the gods who had carried us this far, and then up the river we sailed, until the city of Aea, capital of the land of Colchis, lay before us on the left. On our right was the sacred grove of great close-ranked trees where the serpent-guarded Golden Fleece was hanging, as it had hung since the arrival of Phrixus in Colchis, on the branches of a leafy oak. It was the fiftieth day since we had set sail from Pasagae.

Of our arrival in Colchis, of Jason's involvement with the witch Medea, and of our theft of the Golden Fleece itself, I will try to make a brief telling, since the tale is all so familiar. You will already know how cautious Jason decided not to approach King Aietes at once, for the sons of Phrixus had advised him that Aietes was a dark-souled, dangerous man. Instead Jason ordered us to put the *Argo* into a sheltered marshy backwater while we discussed the strategy he had in mind. And so we lowered and stowed the sail and yard, and unstepped the mast and lay it beside them, and amidst that reedy, stinking, sweltering marsh we came together in council to hear our captain's plan.

Trying to seize the wondrous Fleece by force was obviously impossible. It would be just a sparse handful of us against a whole city. What Jason proposed to do was to take the same simple, straightforward approach with Aietes that he had taken in Iolcus that time when, placing his trust in the gods, he went before his usurping uncle Pelias and asked that he restore the rightful king Aeson to his throne. He meant now to go to Aietes and request that the Fleece be given to him as a sign of favor, because he was the kinsman of Phrixus who had brought the Fleece to Colchis in the first place and an oracle had foretold that it was his destiny to return the Fleece to the land of Phrixus' people.

It was a simple plan indeed, too simple, and there was no reason why it should succeed. Hera, Jason's patron goddess,

s heart must have been downcast upon hearing of all that
etes required of him.

Well, you know the story. That day Eros had struck Jason
th his shaft at his first view of Medea, and had smitten
edea in the same way; and what had passed between them
that moment was the same fiery thing that had passed
tween Eurydice and me, a burning pain so sweet that the
art overflows with it, a force so great that it cannot be with-
od. Jason had felt that force more than once before—you
ll recall that when we were at Lemnos he had nearly let the
hole purpose of our voyage slip from his mind, so infatuated
s he with that island's queen—but for virginal Medea all
is was new, and it took full possession of her soul. Of Jason's
nly magnificence—and he was, in truth, a man of great
d heroic beauty, almost godlike in his strength and splen-
r—she would from that moment on think day and night,
the exclusion of all else. And he too became obsessed with
r: by a mighty oath he swore to make her his wife once he
d succeeded in his quest. But he respected her maidenhood
d did not at that time let the overwhelming desire he felt
r her carry him away. There were great tasks to be done first,
d they both understood how risky it would be to let Aietes
rceive that Jason and his daughter were forming a league
ainst him.

For then and there, linked as they were by the sud-
n bond of passion, Medea and Jason had silently made a
mpact with each other to work together to fulfill Aietes'
quests, and to take the Fleece from him after that. I
ve said that she was a witch and a priestess of mysterious
ecate, and indeed she was. All manner of skills were at

had indeed caused Pelias to greet Jason pleasantly and pretend
to accede to his request, but then Pelias had sent him off on
this voyage, where he might have lost his life a hundred times.
Aietes, I knew, would do the same. To me, for whom the future
is an aspect of the past and the present is an eternal reality,
the outcome was clear: Jason would gain the Fleece, yes, but
not in the easy way he hoped for. But I kept silent and the men
voted their approval of Jason's scheme without hesitation.

So Jason, with the four sons of Phrixus as his guides, went
unarmed from the *Argo* into the city of Aea and presented
himself before Aietes, King of Colchis. With them also went
the wise Peleus and his noble brother Telamon. I was not
there; what I know of Jason's first audience with the king, I
know only by the reports I had from others. But I think it is a
fair rendition of the things that took place.

This Aea was then among the greatest of cities. A high
wall surrounded it, fashioned of smooth well-squared stones of
such immense size that only giants or gods could have hoisted
them into place, and within it stood a royal palace as grand
as any that any king had ever had. Indeed it was as splendid
as the palace of Pharaoh in sun-smitten Egypt, where I had
spent so many years learning the ancient magic of that land.
Egyptian sorcerers had come long ago to Aea, too, bringing
their wisdom and teaching it, and in front of Aea's palace, an
imposing marble structure with cornices of bronze, were great
pillars inscribed with long passages in the secret writing of
Egypt, though I think that in Aietes' time no citizen of Aea
still remembered how to read them. Behind them stood a row
of white stone columns entwined with vines, and four awesome
fountains, which, so the people of Colchis firmly maintain, had

been built for some ancient king of their land by none other than Hephaestus. Indeed they were godly in their majesty, those fountains, one giving forth clear water, and the next one milk, and another oil, and the fourth one wine, gushing freely into basins of iron, bronze, silver, and gold.

Jason and his companions were met first, as he told us afterward, by Chalciope, the king's daughter, who had been the wife of Phrixus. She was surprised to see her sons returning so soon from their voyage to Thessaly; but they simply told her that they had come back to aid Jason in his quest for the Fleece, and forthwith she brought Jason before the king to make his request.

Aietes was then a man of great age, white-haired and bent, but his green eyes were unfaded and keen, and they had a tiger's ferocity. Beside him on his throne was his second wife, Eidyia by name, with her son the prince Apsyrtus at her side. Also there was the witch-priestess Medea, who like Chalciope was Aietes' daughter by his dead first wife. This Medea was a golden-haired woman, very beautiful, with skin of a dark olive hue very strange for one so fair-haired; she had her father's penetrating green eyes, and her brows were heavy and closely knitted together, as though some hidden anger forever raged within her.

The sight of Phrixus' sons back at his court once more drove Aietes instantly to fury. He thought that they had returned with the intent of seizing his throne, bringing some dangerous stranger with them, and coldly ordered them gone, telling them that he would have had their tongues torn out and their hands lopped off, but that they once had dined at his table. Jason, though, stepped calmly forward. You are in no

peril, neither from the sons of Phrixus nor from [...] he said, for they are merely acting as my guide [...] come here only to fulfill the decree of the oracl[...] the return of the Golden Fleece. He told Aietes [...] had brought with him a band of heroes. Peleus a[...] here, were just two of them, and they both cou[...] ancestry back to Zeus; and many another man of [...] was of godly descent as well. He and those who h[...] him would perform any service Aietes might rec[...] by way of compensation for the Fleece—for exam[...] some hostile tribe that stood in need of conques[...]

AS Jason should have understood, Aietes had n[...] to hand over the Fleece than he would have ha[...] crown to the first passing beggar who asked for it[...] kept his own counsel and, though I suspect he[...] to have Jason taken off and slain on the spo[...] an amiable guise and told him that he might w[...] Fleece upon him if Jason and his band would [...] one or two little tasks for him. It was much th[...] that Pelias of Iolcus had adopted when Jason ha[...] to ask him to abdicate. The little tasks Aietes[...] were as hazardous as the voyage to Colchis was—[...] conquering of nearby troublesome tribes, but als[...] involving fire-breathing bulls that needed to [...] plow, and the slaying of certain invincible war[...] from dragons' teeth, and other such well-ni[...] enterprises. Jason maintained a sturdy facade, had indeed caused Pelias to greet Jason pleasantly and pretend to accede to his request, but then Pelias had sent him off on this voyage, where he might have lost his life a hundred times. Aietes, I knew, would do the same. To me, for whom the future is an aspect of the past and the present is an eternal reality, the outcome was clear: Jason would gain the Fleece, yes, but not in the easy way he hoped for. But I kept silent and the men voted their approval of Jason's scheme without hesitation.

So Jason, with the four sons of Phrixus as his guides, went unarmed from the *Argo* into the city of Aea and presented himself before Aietes, King of Colchis. With them also went the wise Peleus and his noble brother Telamon. I was not there; what I know of Jason's first audience with the king, I know only by the reports I had from others. But I think it is a fair rendition of the things that took place.

This Aea was then among the greatest of cities. A high wall surrounded it, fashioned of smooth well-squared stones of such immense size that only giants or gods could have hoisted them into place, and within it stood a royal palace as grand as any that any king had ever had. Indeed it was as splendid as the palace of Pharaoh in sun-smitten Egypt, where I had spent so many years learning the ancient magic of that land. Egyptian sorcerers had come long ago to Aea, too, bringing their wisdom and teaching it, and in front of Aea's palace, an imposing marble structure with cornices of bronze, were great pillars inscribed with long passages in the secret writing of Egypt, though I think that in Aietes' time no citizen of Aea still remembered how to read them. Behind them stood a row of white stone columns entwined with vines, and four awesome fountains, which, so the people of Colchis firmly maintain, had been built for some ancient king of their land by none other than Hephaestus. Indeed they were godly in their majesty, those fountains, one giving forth clear water, and the next one milk, and another oil, and the fourth one wine, gushing freely into basins of iron, bronze, silver, and gold.

Jason and his companions were met first, as he told us afterward, by Chalciope, the king's daughter, who had been the wife of Phrixus. She was surprised to see her sons returning so soon from their voyage to Thessaly; but they simply told her that they had come back to aid Jason in his quest for the Fleece, and forthwith she brought Jason before the king to make his request.

Aietes was then a man of great age, white-haired and bent, but his green eyes were unfaded and keen, and they had a tiger's ferocity. Beside him on his throne was his second wife, Eidyia by name, with her son the prince Apsyrtus at her side. Also there was the witch-priestess Medea, who like Chalciope was Aietes' daughter by his dead first wife. This Medea was a golden-haired woman, very beautiful, with skin of a dark olive hue very strange for one so fair-haired; she had her father's penetrating green eyes, and her brows were heavy and closely knitted together, as though some hidden anger forever raged within her.

The sight of Phrixus' sons back at his court once more drove Aietes instantly to fury. He thought that they had returned with the intent of seizing his throne, bringing some dangerous stranger with them, and coldly ordered them gone, telling them that he would have had their tongues torn out and their hands lopped off, but that they once had dined at his table. Jason, though, stepped calmly forward. You are in no peril, neither from the sons of Phrixus nor from me, is what he said, for they are merely acting as my guides and I have come here only to fulfill the decree of the oracle concerning the return of the Golden Fleece. He told Aietes also that he had brought with him a band of heroes. Peleus and Telamon, here, were just two of them, and they both could trace their ancestry back to Zeus; and many another man of his company was of godly descent as well. He and those who had come with him would perform any service Aietes might require of them by way of compensation for the Fleece—for example, subduing some hostile tribe that stood in need of conquest.

AS Jason should have understood, Aietes had no more desire to hand over the Fleece than he would have had to offer his crown to the first passing beggar who asked for it. But the king kept his own counsel and, though I suspect he was tempted to have Jason taken off and slain on the spot, he assumed an amiable guise and told him that he might well bestow the Fleece upon him if Jason and his band would first carry out one or two little tasks for him. It was much the same tactic that Pelias of Iolcus had adopted when Jason had come to him to ask him to abdicate. The little tasks Aietes had in mind were as hazardous as the voyage to Colchis was—not only the conquering of nearby troublesome tribes, but also some things involving fire-breathing bulls that needed to be yoked to a plow, and the slaying of certain invincible warriors spawned from dragons' teeth, and other such well-nigh impossible enterprises. Jason maintained a sturdy facade, though surely his heart must have been downcast upon hearing of all that Aietes required of him.

Well, you know the story. That day Eros had struck Jason with his shaft at his first view of Medea, and had smitten Medea in the same way; and what had passed between them in that moment was the same fiery thing that had passed between Eurydice and me, a burning pain so sweet that the heart overflows with it, a force so great that it cannot be withstood. Jason had felt that force more than once before—you will recall that when we were at Lemnos he had nearly let the whole purpose of our voyage slip from his mind, so infatuated was he with that island's queen—but for virginal Medea all this was new, and it took full possession of her soul. Of Jason's manly magnificence—and he was, in truth, a man of great and heroic beauty, almost godlike in his strength and splendor—she would from that moment on think day and night, to the exclusion of all else. And he too became obsessed with her: by a mighty oath he swore to make her his wife once he had succeeded in his quest. But he respected her maidenhood and did not at that time let the overwhelming desire he felt for her carry him away. There were great tasks to be done first, and they both understood how risky it would be to let Aietes perceive that Jason and his daughter were forming a league against him.

For then and there, linked as they were by the sudden bond of passion, Medea and Jason had silently made a compact with each other to work together to fulfill Aietes' requests, and to take the Fleece from him after that. I have said that she was a witch and a priestess of mysterious Hecate, and indeed she was. All manner of skills were at her command, the use of magical herbs, of poisons, of spells. Then, too, not only was her heart consumed with love for Jason, but it had long been full of hatred for her father Aietes and his city, for he had neglected her grievously after her mother's death, and she had lived in his palace almost as a maidservant might, embittered and forlorn, a lonely, forgotten woman whose only solace lay in the dark cult of her mistress the moon-goddess Hecate. So with her sister Chalciope's help she had herself secretly conveyed to Jason a little while afterward, and offered him the aid of her witchcraft in performing the tasks that Aietes had laid upon him, and so it was agreed.

When Jason had dealt with the fire-breathing bulls and the magical warriors who had to be overcome, and so forth, making use of a potion Medea had brewed from the blood-red juice of the crocus flower that blooms in the Caucasus in the places where the blood of the tortured Prometheus has spilled, he ordered the *Argo* brought from its hiding-place in the marsh. That was no easy task for us, pulling the vessel free of the heavy muck into which it had settled. We anchored it at a wharf in the city harbor in a place called "the Ram's Couch."

Aietes, ever suspicious, was dismayed at the sight of the great craft and its formidable band of heroes. He was certain now that Jason had come to Colchis to overthrow him. When the news was brought to him soon after that Jason had achieved all that he had been ordered to accomplish, the king was consumed by a high fury and resolved that he would put the *Argo* to the torch and slaughter all her crew, rather than keep his promise to surrender the Fleece.

Unaware, though, of all that had passed betwen Jason and Medea, Aietes was injudicious enough to let slip something to her concerning his intentions. Hastily Medea carried word of that to Jason, telling him that he must seize the Fleece that very night—she would aid him in that, she told him, using one of her potions to lull the serpent that kept watch over it—and then he must set out to sea immediately thereafter. She would, she said, leave Colchis with us, for she was confident that Jason would make good on his pledge to take her as his wife once the expedition had returned to the Hellene lands.

"So be it," said Jason, buckling on his sword.

Then Medea turned to me and said, "You must come along with us today, Orpheus. My drug alone will not be sufficient to close the serpent's eyes."

I understood. Indeed, I had been expecting the request.

So we set out together in the darkness, Jason and Medea and I, toward the sacred forest called the Precinct of Ares, some six miles away from our mooring-place. There the fabled Golden Fleece hung all agleam from a bough of a gigantic oak tree. It was near to dawn when we got there; and when the first pink glow fell upon us out of the east, we beheld not only the tree and the wondrous dazzling Fleece, so bright even in that early light that the eye could barely stand to look upon it for long, but also saw the terrible guardian of the Fleece, lying coiled in casual heaps about the base of the tree, a monstrous mottled green-and-gray thing so thick around that I doubt that even Heracles could have encompassed its girth with his arms.

The snake was sleeping when we approached. But it sensed us quickly, opening first one chilly red-rimmed eye and then the other, and lifted its enormous head and hissed a warning to us to be gone. "By Hera," said Jason in a hoarse whisper, "it would be greater in length than the *Argo* itself, if it uncoiled," and I looked at him and saw him pale and bloodless, with unmistakable terror showing on his face, a thing which I had never seen before. I realized that he must believe now that everything he had struggled for all these many months was slipping from his grasp in this one moment, for surely it would be impossible to gain the mastery over this stupendous monster.

But Medea showed us then, as she would on many occasions thereafter, that she was a woman born without any sense of fear. She went forward until she stood face to face with the beast, so close that she could almost have reached out and tapped it on its scaly snout. It hissed once more and, slowly, almost lazily, drew its huge jaws apart as though it meant to devour her at a gulp. Medea, weaving from side to side very much as if she were a serpent herself, murmured an incantation of some sort, a low rhythmic chant in a language I had never heard before. From the bosom of her gown she drew a small green phial sealed with a waxen stopper and broke the seal, and with a quick gesture splashed the potion that the phial contained across the serpent's slitted nostrils.

A different kind of hiss came from the serpent then, a muzzy soft-edged sound that seemed almost like one of bafflement. A mist came over those hard ophidian eyes and the great eyelids began to grow slack and the beast's head swayed sleepily from one side to the other. But its fanged jaws were still gaping, and even as the creature struggled against the power of Medea's drug it thrust its head malevolently in Jason's direction as though it meant to snap him in two if it could manage to reach him.

"Now," she cried. "Play, Orpheus! Play!"

Yes. I played.

There is music to stir the soul and make a man leap forward eagerly to his death on the battlefield, and there is music to spur the oarsmen of a great ship to pull against the angriest of seas, and there is music that can soothe any creature into the trance of utmost peace. I knew my task and I had the skill. I took my lyre in my hands and from it came such tones as even a monster like this could not withstand. The shallow drowsiness that Medea's potion had induced became deep slumber. The ponderous jaws slowly closed and the huge head sagged and sagged again, until it fell nestling into the creature's tangled coils. I swear by bright-eyed Athena and her father the lord of thunder that the thing had begun to snore.

Quickly Jason broke free of his terrors, sprang forward past the helpless serpent, reached up and pulled the Fleece from the tree. In that same moment the dawning sun came fully into the sky and its brilliant radiance, striking against the Fleece like a bolt of lightning, lit Jason from head to foot so that he seemed to shine with a golden flame. For an instant it seemed that I was looking not upon the mortal son of Aeson but on Apollo himself.

"Come," he cried hoarsely, and we fled from that grove and hurried back to the *Argo* where it lay in harbor. There Jason displayed his glittering prize to our astonished comrades, who gathered round, murmuring in awe. Medea came aboard with us, as she had said she would. We said the words that we hoped would bring the restless spirit of dead Phrixus on board too, for that was part of our task. That having been done, we cut our hawsers then and there, and with a furious splashing of oars we pulled out into the open water.

13
Thirteen

I T WAS NOT so much in our seizing of the Fleece but in our homeward journey to Hellas that we felt the full weight of the test that the gods had devised for us. Nothing we had suffered on the outward trip, however grueling it had seemed at the time, appeared in hindsight to have offered any real difficulty at all when placed against what we had to contend with on the voyage home.

You may think that all we had to do was reverse our track and sail back through now-familiar waters, down the Euxine to the Bosphorus, down the Bosphorus to the Hellespont, and quickly onward by way of the ports we had visited on the way out to our starting-point at Pasagae. But that was not to be. The seer Phineus had advised us to take another route, going counterclockwise around the upper end of the Euxine and down a large unknown westward-flowing river that we would eventually come to, and thence onward by a roundabout course into our native seas. For the current and the winds would be against us if we attempted to sail southward through the Euxine, he warned us, and, what was even worse, all the nations that dwelled along that route were subject in one way or another to King Aietes of Colchis. The enraged Aietes was sure to send out messengers to them, ordering them to intercept us and take us, along with his traitorous daughter and our stolen booty, back to Aea.

In fact Aietes, driven not merely to rage but almost to madness when the news of the theft of the Fleece was brought to him, lost no time sending a fleet out in pursuit of us, an armada of many swift warships headed by his son the prince Apsyrtus, Medea's half-brother. While we were groping our way slowly and uncertainly westward through the upper waters of the Euxine, with our helmsman Ancaeus hard pressed to navigate in a sea where neither he nor any of the rest of us had had any experience, the fleet of Apsyrtus, traveling in its home territory, was making haste to overtake us. Hardly had we reached the entrance to that great river of which Phineus had told us but we saw his ships coming up to surround us. There were Colchian vessels all about us, fifteen or perhaps twenty of them, blocking our access to the river and cutting off our access to the sea as well. We stood on the verge of a one-sided battle, the slaughter of many men, unburied ghosts left to wander in these strange seas. Surely that was not what the gods had had in mind when they sent us on this journey; but wherever we looked we could see the spears of Apsyrtus' multitude of warriors bristling in the sun.

Here Jason demonstrated what manner of man he was, and then Medea showed what sort of woman she was, and Apsyrtus revealed his nature as well, and the gods who have made us all surely took pleasure in watching them work out the destinies that had been designed for them. I knew, after a fashion, what was about to happen, but I could not have intervened. The tragedy had to occur. It is always my fate to be a spectator at such events as the one that would now entwine these three people and send them all spinning off to different, but terrible, destinies.

Jason, ever cautious and prudent to a fault, sent word to Apsyrtus that he had an offer to make, and asked for a brief truce while he prepared his message. To this Apsyrtus, young and naive, unwisely agreed. Then Jason called us together and told us of the compromise that he planned to offer the Colchian prince. The Fleece, Jason was going to say, unquestionably belonged to him: King Aietes had promised it to him if he performed certain tasks, the tasks had been performed, and he meant to hold the king to his pledge. But Medea was a different matter. Jason appeared to regard her as a negotiable commodity. He planned to tell Absyrtus that he was willing to put her ashore on a nearby island where there was a shrine of Artemis, and would leave it up to the ruler of that island to decide whether she should be turned over to her brother or allowed to go on to Hellas with him.

Why Jason believed that Apsyrtus, however callow he might be, should have accepted any such offer, is nothing that I will ever understand. Plainly Aietes had charged him with regaining the Fleece, and he could not trade it away. But that Medea would lightly go along with the thing that Jason was suggesting was even less likely. Another woman, I suppose, might have heard Jason's words without demur, thinking that it was her role as a woman to accept in placid fashion whatever fate might befall her. But Medea, that dark and ruthless woman, surely would not permit herself to be trifled with this way. Nor did she.

Angrily, her eyes ablaze with green fire, she drew Jason aside and reminded him of the oath he had sworn to take her to wife. Did he now mean to break that oath? Was he so meek and fearful that he was ready now to hand her over to her brother with nothing more than a shrug, merely to save his own neck, if some local king should rule that he must do so? She would set fire to the *Argo* with her own hands before she permitted that, and would call down such vengeful curses on Jason and all his kind for generations to come that he would bemoan the day he had ever been born.

She was a frightening woman when angered, was Medea. And the savage words that she spat at him left the heroic Jason well and truly frightened.

He did what he could to pacify her, vowing that he wanted above all else to live with her as man and wife. But he tried to persuade her that he had no choice but to offer Apsyrtus at least a portion of what he had come here to take. There was no way that Medea could remain with him, he said: either she went peacefully, or Apsyrtus would seize her by force. Jason pointed to the vast armada confronting them, and Apsyrtus' great horde of warriors. Any battle between the men of Colchis and the Argonauts could end only in the total destruction of

Jason and all his shipmates, and in the end Apsyrtus would regain not only the Fleece but Medea herself, whom he would take back to Aea to face the dreadful wrath of her royal father.

"It will not happen that way," Medea said coolly. And she told Jason of the strategem that she intended to follow. She would send a messenger to her brother, informing him that she had been abducted by Jason against her will and yearned to be rescued and restored to her native city and her beloved father. "If you will go to your sister secretly by night on shore," the messenger was to tell Apsyrtus, "she will surrender both herself and the Fleece to you, and you will return in triumph to your father with them both, having lost not so much as a single man of your force."

"And if he does come, what then?" asked Jason.

"You will be waiting in hiding for him, and you will kill him," said Medea, with not the slightest quaver of emotion in her voice. "When they learn of his death his men will be thrown into confusion, and we will be able to escape and go safely onward together to your country."

And so it occurred, and all the dark things that were to happen afterward as well, for the gods had designed all this to occur in just such a way. And what the gods design for us must of necessity come to pass.

I know that philosophers will arise in years to come who will claim that we and we alone are masters of our fates, shaping all events of our lives by our own decisions. They are undoubtedly sincere in this belief; but what chagrin they would feel, if only they understood that the very ideas they espouse were put into their minds by Father Zeus, as part of his great plan for the cosmos and all creatures that dwell within it?

So the foolish Apsyrtus went unescorted to the temple of Artemis on shore, where Medea had said she would be waiting for him with the Golden Fleece. She came forth to meet him in the darkness; but as brother and sister stood there quietly talking, Jason emerged from his hiding place behind the temple and struck Apsyrtus dead with his sword. His spurting blood threw a crimson stain over the silvery veil Medea had donned. But grim Medea, unmoved, took the sword from Jason, cut the dead man's body in pieces, and cast his sundered limbs into the sea, where the Colchians would find them drifting in the morning; and she and Jason returned in silence to the *Argo*.

As Medea had foreseen, the Colchians lost all heart after the death of their prince. Fearing the fury of Aietes if they returned empty-handed to Aea, they set sail for the farther shores of the Euxine and built new settlements there for themselves and never were heard from again. We, meanwhile, entered the great river unhindered and traveled onward toward the west.

But the gods in their mysterious wisdom often lead us into preordained inevitable sin and then implacably demand atonement. Hera still looked kindly on her beloved Jason, but Zeus, who had never shown any friendship for Jason, was of another mind entirely. And so, the goddess aiding us as best she could but the angry father-god insisting that a proper price be paid for the crime that had made possible our escape, the rest of our journey was one torment after another, by way of punishment for Medea's crime and Jason's acquiescence in it, until Medea was deemed cleansed of her brother's blood.

We sailed up that uncharted westward-flowing river through bitter lands of ice and snow, shivering in northern gales that slowed the very course of our blood. The oarsmen's hands froze as they gripped the oars. Storms assailed us and came close to shattering our mast. Huge deadly floating masses of ice came drifting all about us, jutting up far above us and making every day seem like a running of the Clashing Rocks. We grew gaunt and weak with hunger, but Ancaeus did wondrous deeds at the helm and I beat time for the weary men with whatever energy remained in me, and we managed to go on.

Deep in the heart of the continent we found at last another mighty river, likewise unknown then to any Hellene mariner, that rose somewhere at the world's end and flowed southward into our own broad-breasted ocean. When we emerged finally into a place of warmer weather, new storms caught us and spun us around, driving us northward again past the coast of what we surmised was Italy. We fought our way south once more, entering at last into the Tyrrhenian Sea that we knew would take us back to the Hellene lands, only to find ourselves confronted by the isle where the Sirens dwelled, those seductive singers who are put there to lure mariners to their destruction. "There is no other way for us," said Ancaeus, "but to go past their shore. But who can resist the Sirens' song?"

Well, I had sung three-headed Cerberus into pleasant slumber, and I had soothed the serpent guardian of the Fleece the same way, and now I took lyre in hand to get us past this peril as well, for I knew that other tasks awaited me beyond this voyage and we were not destined to end our days here.

THESE Sirens are my cousins, daughters of my mother's sister Terpsichore the muse. Their voices are clear and beautiful, and when travelworn seamen pass their island they sing out in chorus, beckoning them ashore to supposed delights, but actually intending their deaths. They offer soft bosoms and a warm resting-place to weary travelers, and few can say no to them.

But I know a little about the art of song myself; and as the Sirens began their lovely song, I cut across it with a rousing chanty of my own that entirely canceled out their alluring harmonies, breaking over them and engulfing them in robust manly rhythms. I sang to the oarsmen of all that we had endured, and all that we had achieved, and of how close we were now to home and the glory that awaited us upon our return. My song lifted their spirits, and, exhausted and famished though they were, they pulled hard at their oars, and the Sirens were powerless to make themselves heard above my voice and the steady thrumming of my lyre. Only one of our number, young Butes of Iolcus, was able to tune his ear to their song instead of mine, and leaped overboard and swam on toward shore, where those devilish sisters pounced upon him in the surf.

To Sicily then we came, King Alcinous' realm. There we were met with a welcoming feast. But even as we rejoiced in this comfort after our hard voyage, dark sails appeared off shore: yet another fleet of Colchis, sent out by Aietes to rove the seas in search of Medea and the Fleece. Of course they could not attack us while we were Alcinous' guests; but the Colchian envoy who went before the king accused us of theft and worse, and asked Alcinous to turn over to them all that we had stolen from their king. And Alcinous, fearing to make an enemy of Aietes and unwilling also to bring the wrath of thundering Zeus upon himself, showed a willingness to do so.

Jason was unable to refute these accusations, and was helpless and baffled here. But Medea stood up boldly before the king and begged for mercy from him, pleading with him not to separate her from Jason, whom the gods had destined for her as her mate. Surely, she said, her father, who had never loved her and now looked upon her as a traitor, would put her to death if she were brought back to Colchis. Did Alcinous, that wise and generous king, mean to send a guest of his household to such a death?

Alcinous was moved by her tender words, just as Jason, earlier, had been swayed by her angry ones. The king declared that if she was still a virgin, he would indeed send her back to Aietes, for Aietes had a father's right to her and Jason had none at all. But if Medea and Jason were married, he would not come between a husband and his wife. That night we poured the wine and honey for the gods, and sacrificed the sheep, and built a wedding bed for Jason and Medea with the Golden Fleece spread upon it as a coverlet; and so, in haste, their marriage was consummated in this foreign land instead of in Jason's father's house in Iolcus, as he had intended. It may have been a happy night for them but there would be little happiness for these two in the years ahead.

Concerning the remainder of our long time of tribulations I will be brief. When we left Sicily we were caught by a

northerly gale and blown toward sun-parched Africa, into the
Gulf of Libya, where our ship was caught by one of the wild
tides of that place and carried far up onto the desert shore.
Ancaeus the helmsman gave way to grief at this; for not only
were we beached, but he knew that when the tide returned it
would sweep us just as irresistibly out upon the rocky shoals
that rose everywhere in this desolate place, and our hull would
be shattered beyond hope of repair. So there was no alternative for us but to take the terrible weight of the *Argo* upon
our backs, lifting the ship and hauling it across the desert,
day after brutal day, an effort that very nearly was beyond our
ability. At last, just as we were coming to the last of our endur-
ance, we reached navigable waters beyond. No suffering in all
the time since we had first set out was equal to the suffering
that this portage imposed on us; and we were weeping tears
of blood by the time we staggered at last to the brink of a
brackish lake and put the *Argo*'s keel into water once more.

To the open sea we sailed, and thence to Crete, and by
one way and another we made our way homeward. You will
know that Jason took the Fleece and his bride to Pasagae,
where there was great rejoicing. Even King Pelias, he who had
sent Jason on the long quest, pretended to be pleased at his
return with the Fleece. Old Aeson, Jason's father, had died
during his absence. Medea, who by then was with child by
Jason, charmed Pelias into believing that she could through
her witchcraft make him young again, but that monstrous
woman gave him poison instead of some magic elixir, so that
he perished in a terrible way and Jason became king in Iolcus.
After which, as you know, he strayed from Medea in his affec-
tions, embracing Glauce, the daughter of the Theban king;

but fierce vengeful Medea slew not only Glauce but her own two young children, leaving only their corpses for Jason, and fled from Thessaly to many other dark exploits elsewhere, of which I need not sing here. And the last years of splendid Jason were blackened by grief and shame.

As for me, I left the *Argo* in the Peloponnese and undertook a pilgrimage to Hades' gate at Tainaron, that place where I had parted forever from my Eurydice. A commandment had been laid upon me to offer up a ceremony of thanksgiving there to the gods for my safe return, which I duly performed, asking no questions. And then finally I went back to Thrace, where the gods meant me to resume my responsibilities as a teacher and a leader, and eventually to meet my doom.

14

fourteen

I DWELLED IN THRACE for a good many years,
then, continuing the work among the harsh and rude
Ciconians that I had begun before Cheiron summoned me off
to the voyage for the Fleece, and I achieved much that was use-
ful in bringing them toward civilization. Not that I remained
there constantly, for an oracle I had consulted had warned me
that a kind of restlessness would overcome me from time to
time and, with nothing more than my lyre and the sack upon
my back, I must get myself off to some distant land and take part
in whatever sacred Mysteries were celebrated there. Such journeys were all part of my task. To fulfill my role in maintaining
the great harmony of the universe I must go from place to place
as I am told, either to teach or just to sing and play, as is needed.

During one of these absences the great war broke out between Hellas and Troy. I need not sing that tale here, the story of Agamemnon and Menelaus and Helen and Paris and Achilles and Hector and all the rest, for others have sung it as well as any mortal ever could. When all that was happening I was far away, visiting Egypt once more—a new Pharaoh ruled there now, a shriveled, fleshless boy whose soul was as dry as the desert sounds of his kingdom. He showed no sign of mortal emotion whatever and wore his double crown like the aegis of a god. This king wanted none of my songs and would have sent me away, though after a time he relented and let me stay, and even had me shown into the richly painted underground chamber where the Pharaoh whom I had known now lay buried amid all his lavish treasures.

Pharaoh's priests shared much arcane wisdom with me, and I stayed with them for several years, to my great benefit, until finally an inner voice told me it was time to go, that the course of my destiny would now take me elsewhere. So back I went to rugged mountain-girt Thrace again. There I learned that while I was still in Egypt, renewing my studies in the lore of that ancient land, the war at Troy had ended and Odysseus of Ithaca, the wily son of my old *Argo* shipmate Laertes, had put ashore at my capital city of Ismarus in the early days of his long voyage home. And Odysseus had let his men sack the place, so that I found much of it wrecked upon my return.

Well, it is the will of the gods that the fortunes of cities ebb and flow; and so I led my people in a great rebuilding, and soon we had the place restored again. Then I considered the work of the spirit that still remained for me to do among the Ciconians. Thrace was then, as it had always been, under the thrall of the violent god Dionysus, who brings the frenzy of madness to men. It is well known that I myself have been sworn all my days to the tranquility and sanity of great Apollo, and I saw it as my duty to bring my people over to Apollo's noble creed, a difficult task indeed. Now, though, I had new knowledge that I could employ. In the course of my second visit to Egypt it had become clear to me that Dionysus and Apollo are merely different aspects of the same divinity, the two sides of the image in the mirror, and I hoped to make use of that revelation as a force for the conversion of my people. But the work went slowly. The Ciconians loved their wild god.

I was interrupted now and again in my task by that restlessness of which I have spoken. On one of those journeys I encountered tireless Odysseus, ever a rover himself, who in the autumn of his years, gray-bearded and bent with age, his once-bright eyes now dimmed and his burly shoulders rounded and slumping, had left his home and wife in Ithaca to roam the world as so often he had done in his stormy youth. We met—by chance, some might say, though I know otherwise—in a tavern in Athens, the city that Theseus had founded in Attica. "The seer Teiresias told me," he said, "that I would make one more voyage in my old age, though he did not tell me where I would go. But Poseidon, who visits me by night in dreams that shake my bed, will give me no rest until I do."

He was thinking of going to Egypt, he said. But I saw nothing promising for that crafty man in so staid and rigid a land. He would only break himself against the immovable hieratic stillness of that unchanging place. Instead I urged him toward the west, toward the undiscovered realms beyond the sunset. What you have always chosen to do, I told him, was to follow knowledge like a sinking star, beyond the utmost bound of human thought; and that is what you must do again on this new and final voyage of yours. As I spoke, an unearthly light entered his eyes, which took on again all that eagerness and hunger for experience that had driven him in earlier times, and the years seemed to drop away from him so that he seemed once more to be the potent far-seeing leader whose sagacity and guile had guided the Hellenes so well in their war against Priam's Troy.

So I went to sea with Odysseus. He bought a ship in Athens—it was not nearly so fine as the *Argo*, but it would do—and put up postings for crewmen—they flocked to his banner, not a band of heroes such as the Argonauts had been, but good enough for the job—and westward off we went, past the isles of Hellas, past Italy, into the unknown.

Early in the journey he spoke to me, of his own accord, of the sacking of my city. "The wind," he said, "drove us from Troy to your Ismarus, and we came ashore very hungry and badly in need of fresh water. You know how that is. As you might guess, we weren't greeted with any sort of friendliness. But we had just come from the destruction of a much greater city than yours and were full of a sense of our own strength, and so we fell upon your Ciconians and took from them by force what they wouldn't give us out of generosity. You know how it is."

"I know how it is, yes."

"But then"—and such a look of great sadness and regret came into those cunning eyes that for a moment I could almost believe was a genuine show of his feelings—"then,

after swilling too much wine and slaughtering too many
sheep, my foolish men turned mutinous and began to loot the
city and seize the women, and nothing I could say would hold
them back. How that angered me, to see them running wild
that way!"

I **UNDERSTOOD** then that look of regret that had come
into his eyes: what proud Odysseus regretted was not so much
the sack of my city, for which he made no apology, but rather
the shameful fact that he had been unable to control his own
men. He went on to tell me how the Ciconians had summoned their kinsmen from outlying districts and driven him
and his men away, though not before much damage had been
done. "Many of your people died. I lost some dozens of my
own. And so it went. It is the way of the gods to engineer such
calamities for us."

"The way of the gods, yes," I said. "And so it went."

After that Odysseus and I spoke no more of the sack
of Ismarus.

We kept Africa on our left as we sailed, and the coast of
the Hesperian lands on our right, and in time we found ourselves passing through the Pillars of Heracles and staring at the
great uncharted sea that lies beyond them. Odysseus' weary
men began to mutter at the sight of that endless expanse of
water and talked of turning back. But he called them together
and said, "Brothers, you who have passed through a hundred
thousand perils to reach this place, do not deny yourself this
last exploit. Here lies a chance to learn for yourself what lies in

this unknown world on the far side of the sun, where no people dwell." Who could resist the force of that man? He pointed toward the northwest; and all muttering ceased, and they put their shoulders to the oars, and toward the northwest we went.

So we came to the Hyperborean lands of snow and ice, and of course they were not uninhabited at all, but were home to a race of tall fair-skinned golden-haired folk. We coasted there awhile, until the unending darkness of the winter drove even long-enduring Odysseus to despair; then we turned west and found an island not quite as bleak and snowy, where we made a landing and visited with its people, who were dark and stocky but did not look at all like us, and traveled far inland to a place where they had their temple, one that was not in any way like the temples of Hellas: it was just a double ring of huge lofty stones, with equally huge crosspieces laid atop them as lintels.

The people of the island were very proud of this temple, which must have been built by giants or magicians. At first they would not let us look on while they celebrated their rites there, but then I played my lyre for them and sang, and told of the secret things in a way that showed them that all gods are the same god, and when they saw that my music obeyed the laws of the harmony of the universe they let us take part in their ceremony. It was a very strange one indeed. I will not speak of it except to say that it left me with a feeling of deep fulfillment, seeing as I did that the eternal truths held sway even here at the end of the earth.

And afterward? We sailed out into the ocean again and would have gone southward until the stars we knew had slipped below the horizon and we entered the fabled fiery territories beyond the rim of the world. But storms came up and our vessel was whirled round and round until it seemed we would be carried to the bottom; and although we survived it, brave Odysseus at last was unable to make his men carry us any farther, and perhaps, though he would never have admitted it, he had come finally to the end of his own hunger for exploration. So we turned back and searched for the entrance to our own sea, a sea that we Hellenes think is great in size but now seemed to us small and almost comical after the one on whose breast we had been traveling so long, and to Hellas we returned. Of Odysseus I heard nothing more. I think he died in his own bed in Ithaca, all his questing finally at an end. My own death, which, as I knew, awaited me in Thrace, was not nearly so peaceful.

15

fifteen

SINCE EARLIEST TIMES, as I have said, the people of Thrace have worshipped the god Dionysus. Now you must know that Dionysus is an aspect of the One God, as Apollo is also, and thundering Zeus, and Poseidon of the trident and dark Hades and white-armed Hera and Aphrodite and Athena and all the rest; and they are all divine in their own ways, but each of us must choose that aspect of divinity which speaks to his own mind and soul, and make that the focus of our worship. Or, rather, each of us is chosen by some aspect of divinity. I had from birth belonged to Apollo; but my Ciconian people belonged to Dionysus, that roaring god, that god of blood and wine and fire.

Now the worship of Dionysus is valuable up to a point, as the worship of any god is valuable. Through his Mysteries it was possible to find that gateway into the deeper reality that is the goal of all worship. I myself had sung songs of the birth of Dionysus, Zeus's son by Persephone, whom Zeus had meant one day to be his own successor. I told how in the early days of the world the Titans, those old sulking overthrown gods, the rebellious children of Uranus, grew jealous of the upstart child's glory and fell upon him and tore him apart, and even fed on the flesh of his sundered limbs, though Athena was able to rescue his heart, from which Zeus caused Dionysus to be born again. Zeus in fury destroyed the Titans then with a thunderbolt, and from their ashes the race of mortal men arose. All this was a story of the eternal cycle of death and rebirth that underlies all existence. Dionysus the immortal god who dies, Dionysus the resurrected, was the spirit of life against which the forces of death unceasingly contend. One sings of such stories, not because they are the literal truth, but because they cast the light of truth over the deep realities of the world.

But, over the years, the Dionysiac cult of my people had grown wilder and bloodier, until its frenzy reached such a crazed pitch that it obscured rather than revealed those truths that all of us strive to comprehend, and truth became imprisoned in that obscurity. It was my task in Thrace to untwist the chains that had come to tie the hidden soul of harmony.

In our land the chief worshippers of the resurrected god were women, who called themselves Bacchantes, for Bacchus was one of Dionsyus' innumerable names, but they also were known as maenads, or raving ones, to those who took them to be madwomen. Certainly their way of giving praise to their god was a ferocious one. Clad in goatskins and bedecking their hair with snakes, they raged wild-eyed through the countryside with painted faces, playing harsh music on shrill flutes, beating on drums and cymbals and jangling tambourines, waving pine torches aloft, uttering piercing bloodcurdling shrieks, ripping apart whatever lay in their path. Their minds were blurred by wine and the fumes of incense, and in their ecstasies they bade farewell entirely to reason and rampaged like an uncheckable force. At the climax of their rites they would fall upon a bull, which they believed to be the incarnation of their Dionysus, and tear the beast asunder with their hands, devouring its raw flesh by way of attaining union with the god.

Often did I see our maenads trooping back afterward from the forest, their cheeks and forearms smeared horribly with the blood of the sacrificed bull. They were already growing calmer, their passions spent, but still were half lost in a transport of holy fervor. The leader of these Bacchantes was named Hesione, my own kinswoman, the daughter of my father's brother. Her perpetual companion was scarlet-haired Phorixo, a woman who stood nearly as tall as any man, and with them often was soft-faced Carya, younger than the other two, a practitioner of the healing arts. In the daily life of the city these women were, all three, tender and loving wives and mothers, adept in the skills of the household, and, as I have said, Carya was also one who could knowledgeably minister to those in pain. But they were devotees of Dionysus as well, and when the fit was on them they were frightening to behold, wholly caught up in the mad rampages by which they honored their god.

"Look at these," I would say to Hesione, showing her the portraits of Dionysus and Apollo that stood in our temple.

"Can you not see that one is the mirror image of the other? These gods are one and the same, Hesione."

"They are nothing like each other," she would reply.

"Each represents one aspect of the whole," I told her then. "Dionysus is fiery energy; Apollo is calmness and sanity. Our goal should be to unite the two in one."

"And have you done that? You ignore Dionysus entirely. You are merely Apollo's creature. And you anger Dionysus greatly, Orpheus, through your neglect of him."

"No," I said. "Not so. In my music I worship him as deeply as you do. My music contains both Apollo and Dionysus, or it would not have the power to move the soul."

She could not be swayed. Her voice was crisp with scorn. "Your music comes entirely from Apollo, whatever you may say. It lacks the fire of Dionysus." And she laughed. "Come with us, some day, to the mountainside, and hear the sounds of our flutes and cymbals and drums, and then you will learn what true music is."

I smiled at that. "I think I know what true music is. And also I know that the true Dionysus is the force of creation, brought to us by Zeus as the bearer of life—not, as you women would have it, of mindless destruction. But let that pass. You say I should come with you to your revels and learn the truth of your beliefs. But do you mean that? Would you really want a man present at your feast, Hesione? Admit it, cousin: when the full madness is upon you, you detest all men, and would tear any man apart who went near you!"

"You say we detest men? You, who loathe all woman-kind so much that you take only handsome youths as your lovers?"

THE LAST SONG OF ORPHEUS

I reminded her of my love for Eurydice, whom I still mourned in songs that made all the world weep. If I had turned to members of my own sex for the comforts of love after the death of Eurydice—and it was true; I had, many times—it was only because no other woman in the world could ever have been to me what Eurydice was. But that in itself only angered Hesione all the more, for she saw it as a rejection of her entire sex. I could do nothing against such a belief. Nor could I pry her loose from her conviction that the Dionysus of the maenad frenzies was the true Dionysus.

I knew, as I have always known, that only by becoming Dionysus myself, only through my dying and being reborn even as he was slain and born again, could I break through the wall of her madness and the madnesses of her cult. By that sacrifice, and by it alone, would I be able to return my people to the essential way of harmony. Gods must die—and there is a part of me that is a god—to lead their people onward to the truth.

I was prepared for it. I had prepared for it all my life. By dying as in their fables Dionysus himself had died, I would become Dionysus for them, and they would worship me as they had worshipped him, and Dionysus and Apollo would at last be united in their minds.

And so—and so—when the day came—"The maenads are dancing in the forest, Orpheus," said one of the men of my court. "You must go to them and calm them with your music, or they will destroy us all!"

"Yes," I said. "I must go to them."

I heard the strident screeching of their flutes long before I saw them, the pounding of their drums, the penetrating outcry. Then they came into view, dozens of them, racing wild-eyed across the meadow, their painted faces shining, their serpent-threaded hair unbound and streaming behind them, their animal-skin garments hanging open. How crazed they were! How far gone in their frenzies, how maddened by love of their god!

Here was beautiful Hesione, face smeared with blood and distorted into a terrible grimace, eyes so glazed she scarcely seemed to recognize me.

"Do you know me, Hesione?" I asked, holding my lyre aloft. "I am Orpheus. Come, Hesione. Listen to my song."

I could tell that she had no idea who I was. She scooped up a strand of ivy and held it beckoningly toward me, as though she meant to bedeck my shoulders with it as one would bedeck a bull being made ready for the sacrifice. From her crimson lips came a strange bellowing sound that no one would know for the voice of a woman.

Beside her at the front of the pack was tall scarlet-haired Phorixo, altogether lost in the raptures of her rite, and next to her gentle Carya the healer, but she was not so gentle now, for the blood of beasts ran down her arms and shoulders, and dripped from the tips of her bared breasts. Carya, at least, knew me. "So there you are, Orpheus! You who scorns us all, come to mock us!"

"You know me, Carya," I said. "I mock no one."

And I took up my lyre and began to play.

The birds in the trees heard my song and ceased their chatter.

The snakes wrapped in the maenads' hair heard me. The wild animals of the forest heard me.

Golden Apollo himself heard me. He hovered in the air above me, visible as though through a bright shimmering veil. He touched his lyre and I heard his music answering mine. And I saw the stars shining by day all about him, pulsing and quivering like drumheads beating of their own accord, filling the heavens with all their many colors, and I heard once more those thousand thousand lyres all at once, and the stars were singing their blessed song, that vast eternal harmony, that celestial music that has ever been my joy.

"Now you know who you are, Orpheus, and who you will be," said Apollo to me, as he had in my boyhood.

I smiled, and I felt the warm glow of his smile upon me.

But the Bacchantes themselves heard only the imagined voice of their god, who was Apollo also, but in the form of fiery Dionysus.

Hesione threw the first stone, which struck me in the forehead. The healer Carya threw the next; and then the air was thick with them, striking hard, knocking the breath from me. I fell to my knees. They came rushing toward me, shrieking.

So it was about to happen, the thing I had seen so many times in my memories of the future, the thing that had happened before and would happen again, and again and again. Well, so be it. It had been decreed. The stones battered me, but I did not stop playing. In another instant the women were swarming around me like hungry beasts. Their deafening shrieks assailed my ears. I felt the blows of their ivy-wrapped staffs. In a moment they would rake my skin with their nails and seize my arms and tear at my flesh.

But I held tight to my lyre and continued to play. I am Orpheus, Apollo's son, and the gods had placed me here for this. So, calling on all the strength that remained to me, I played and I sang. By grace of Apollo, I played and I sang. I would not cease my song until the end. I knew that the time was coming once again for me to die; but it was not here yet, and, until that time had come, I would not cease my song.